GRACE UNDER FURY

FEDERAL BUREAU OF MAGIC COZY MYSTERY, BOOK 4

ANNABEL CHASE

RED PALM PRESS LLC

CHAPTER ONE

"I'LL PUT up the invisibility shield," Neville said. My assistant and I were making the most of a beautiful day by having me kill simulated demons in fresh air and sunshine. All part of my Federal Bureau of Magic training that I failed to get as an agent for the FBI.

"An invisibility shield sounds very superhero-y," I said.

"Indeed." Neville conjured a shield around the training area so that no humans could observe us, unless they possessed the Sight, of course.

"What do I do first?" I asked.

"We'll run through three main exercises," the wizard explained. "You defeat your adversary in each one."

"What if I don't?" I asked.

"These are only simulations," Neville said. "I've designed them so that they can't actually injure you, but try to forget that bit or the training won't work."

"I'm not great at faking it," I said, and was immediately grateful that no family members were within earshot. I could only imagine the comebacks to that statement.

"Best of luck, Agent Fury," Neville said. The wizard

removed a pouch from his pocket and tossed sparkly dust in the air before seeking refuge behind a tree. "Adversary number one!"

"Why are you hiding behind a tree if he's only a fake?" I asked.

The dust swirled in the air and formed a body with grayish skin, horns, and a forked tail.

"He's only a fake, but you're not."

Neville was right to be concerned. As a fury, my powers were of the rare and impressive variety. In every generation, a fury was definitely *not* born. My wicked family thought they'd hit the supernatural jackpot with me. Their DNA hadn't spit out a fury for centuries until I came along. What they didn't anticipate was that I'd choose a righteous path and reject my true nature. When I was younger, they'd assumed it was a form of rebellion. Eventually, they came to realize that I was committed to planting myself firmly in the Garden of Good.

Smoke poured out of the demon's nostrils, snapping me back to attention. I concentrated on his appearance.

Know with whom you're having the pleasure. That's what my former FBI partner Fergus used to say. It made sense as an FBM agent, too, albeit for different reasons.

"Agent Fury!" Neville prompted.

"I'm working on it!" Identification was the first step. "Ugly Guy!"

"That's a description, not an identification," Neville called.

"I know," I said. "I'm just starting off with insults, the way a good agent should."

Neville grinned. "An excellent point, Most Talented One."

"Neville," I warned.

He lowered his head. "Apologies, Agent Fury," he said.

Ugly Guy decided not to wait for me to act. He charged me with his horns and I reached out to grab them.

"Sorry, pal. My dance card is full."

I swung him around and was surprised to find I could lift him without straining a muscle. I knew I was strong, but this seemed a step up from my 'normal' ability. The demon went flying across the grass.

"I give you a 9.3 for form," I yelled.

"Best to identify him in order to defeat him," Neville sang out from behind the tree.

Right. I racked my brain, cataloguing all his visible traits. I was sure I'd read about this demon in the notes Neville had forced upon me. I'd wanted to read about a drug bust in San Francisco that Fergus had been involved in, but Neville reminded me in his kindly way that my place was with the FBM now. I was still adjusting to that unexpected career trajectory.

"Once you know his type, you can identify his weakness," Neville called.

"Okay, backseat wizard," I said. "Stop trying to take the magic wheel."

The demon lumbered toward me and dropped his head, probably preparing to use those horns as a skewer. A bright red spot between the horns caught my eye.

"It's a Target demon," I cried.

"I don't think that exists," Neville said.

I pointed excitedly at the demon's head. "That's what I call it because the spot on its head looks like the Target logo."

"The shop?" Neville asked.

I somersaulted to the side to avoid the demon's attack. "Yes," I said, springing back to my feet. "The real name is a Jupiter demon." It was named after the planet because of their matching red spots.

"That is correct, Agent Fury," Neville said—the most reserved cheerleader in history.

I remembered from Neville's notes that the demon's heart is his weakness. When Jupiter came back into my orbit, I let him come within striking distance. Then I punched a hole straight through his chest and grasped his heart, squeezing it before I wrenched it from his body. The demon screamed and howled in protest before dissipating.

"Nicely done, O' Immortal One," Neville said.

I glared at him. "I told you not to call me that."

"And I told you not to eat cheddar popcorn at your desk because it leaves a trail of yellow powder, nevertheless you persist."

I eyed him. "Cheddar popcorn is amazing."

He ignored me. "Ready for the next one?"

"I think you're enjoying this more than I am."

He stepped out from behind the tree. "It isn't every day I get to utilize my wizarding skills. Paul wasn't keen on any kind of practice sessions. He was more of a desk jockey." Paul Pidcock was my predecessor. His unexpected death by demon was the reason I was here now. I'd had no intention of ever returning to my hometown of Chipping Cheddar, but once the FBI discovered my special abilities, the decision was out of my hands.

"So what level are we up to?" I asked. The training guidelines were designed like a video game, with different milestones to hit.

"Midway through four," Neville said. "You should be quite proud, Agent Fury. You've made excellent progress."

"Enough progress that I've earned an iced latte?" I was all about the carrot over the stick, something my family failed to understand about me.

"I am peckish." He glanced past the river. "Shall we check the portal first, while we're out here?"

"Good idea."

The dormant portal to Otherworld, the supernatural realm, is the main reason for an FBM outpost in Chipping Cheddar. It's located in the hillside adjacent to Davenport Park, known locally as 'the mound.' Due to the portal's mystical energy, the town serves as a magnet for supernaturals in the human world.

Neville removed the invisibility shield and we crossed the park to the mound. The wizard stood sentry while I ducked inside and did a quick sweep of the area. Normal vibrations. Normal energy levels.

"Nothing out of the ordinary," I said, returning to his side.

"I'll write it in the daily report," Neville said.

As we left the mound, a familiar figure appeared on the horizon and my heart jumped. Chief Sawyer Fox sauntered toward us, his snug uniform outlining every muscle on his fit body.

Beside me, Neville squealed and pointed.

"Don't make a big deal," I hissed. "We're playing it cool." As a human and the chief of police in Chipping Cheddar, he was the last person I could get involved with. There'd been a bump in the Road to Disinterest when a supernatural fog had settled over town and made us act out our impulses. Turned out my impulse was to smooch Chief Fox in the men's bathroom at The Cheese Wheel, our local watering hole. The last time I'd seen him was after the fog had lifted. We'd stood in my future home—the barn that straddled the border of my parents' respective properties—and he'd expressed an interest in dating, which I'd begrudgingly shot down. He didn't know about the supernatural world and I had to keep it that way. My world was too dangerous for a human, even one as capable as Sawyer Fox.

"Not the chief," Neville said. "His little friend."

I looked at him askance. "You're excited about a gun?"

Only when Neville rushed forward did I see what the fuss was about. An adorable pug peeked out from behind the chief's leg. I'd been too busy ogling the man to spot his furry companion.

"New recruit for paw patrol?" I asked, once we were within conversational range.

Chief Fox grinned and looked down at the pug. "This is Achilles."

"I wouldn't recommend dipping him in any rivers," I said. "His legs are too short."

"Wouldn't dream of it," the chief said. "Though I am looking forward to teaching him commands. Heel is my particular favorite."

Neville doubled over with laughter. "Good one, Chief."

I looked blankly at my assistant. "So what? Princess Buttercup can do that."

Neville snorted. "Achilles, heel. Get it?"

I rolled my eyes so hard that I was pretty sure I pulled it out of its socket. "Ancient Greek jokes? There's a limited audience for you." I crouched down to pet the friendly pug. He licked my hand like it was covered in steak juice.

"Is this another one of your adoption efforts?" Neville asked. "I have to say, I think it's a stellar idea." Chief Fox had started patrolling with dogs from the local shelter in an effort to help them get adopted. Just one more reason to lust after him.

"Actually, I've decided to adopt Achilles myself," the chief said. "Now that I'm settled here, I figured it was time for a furry friend."

"You've already got Deputy Guthrie," I said. Despite his red hair and fair complexion, Sean Guthrie was surprisingly hairy— a fact I'd inadvertently learned in high school when his butt cheeks were taped together by the wrestling team.

Chief Fox chuckled. "Achilles is more my style."

I resumed a standing position. "You chose well. He's a sweetheart."

"What do you say we get our dogs together one of these days for a play date?" he asked.

"Princess Buttercup might mistake him for a snack." My hellhound was a gentle giant but still a giant, although to humans like Chief Fox, she had the appearance of a Great Dane.

"I was hoping you could show me a few pointers," Chief Fox said. "You've managed to bend a big dog like yours to your will...You must know a few tricks."

I knew exactly what he was trying to do. It would be a way of spending time together without actually dating. Clever. I was sorely tempted to take him up on it.

"I don't think Agent Fury would be very good at that," Neville interjected. He gave me a pointed look.

"Thanks for the vote of confidence, Neville," I said.

"Well, if you change your mind, you know how to reach me." His gaze lingered on me for another moment before he and Achilles continued their patrol.

The moment he was out of earshot, I smacked Neville's arm. "Don't speak for me."

"I had to," he said, rubbing his arm. "You wanted to say yes."

"Of course I did. Did you see that chin dimple?"

Neville heaved a sigh. "Need I remind you...?"

I held up a hand. "You needn't." I'd heard it enough from my family. A relationship with me would put the chief in danger and jeopardize the secrecy of our world. I knew Chief Fox well enough at this point to know he'd want to join the fight against demons, once he'd overcome his shock. He took the whole 'serve and protect' thing very seriously—a quality I liked about him, but also a quality that made a relationship with him impossible. A hapless carpenter like John

7

Maclaren would've been fine. Easy to fool and easy to keep safe. Chief Fox was too sharp and—truth be told—I hated the idea of lying to him. Best to keep him at arm's length.

Neville looked at me with a sympathetic expression. "How about an extra large frappe? My treat."

My assistant knew how to cheer me up. "Whipped cream?"

"I'd be disappointed if you didn't."

I wasn't convinced that whipped cream would cure my Chief Fox blues, but it sure wouldn't hurt to try.

"Ta da!" Neville stood on the pavement outside Magic Beans, the brand new coffee shop in town. I'd ignored the grand opening earlier in the week and I wasn't about to cave now.

"No way," I said. "There's no reason to deviate from The Daily Grind."

"Trust me, Eden," Neville said. "I know how much you love your coffee drinks. I promise you, this place doesn't disappoint."

It wasn't about fear of disappointment. It was about fear of revenge. The proprietor of Magic Beans was none other than Corinne LeRoux, the youngest member of the rival coven in Chipping Cheddar. My family would be apoplectic if they knew I'd spent Fury money in a LeRoux coffee shop. The witches were a tight-knit family and I had no doubt Corinne's mother and grandmother were somehow involved in the business.

The door opened as a customer exited and the aroma of freshly brewed coffee permeated the air. My mouth began to water.

"Is it really better than The Daily Grind?" That was the only coffee shop in town that came anywhere close to the coffee in San Francisco.

Neville leaned over and whispered, "I've been skipping the donuts and coffee at Holes this week just so I can order the triple mint latte at Magic Beans."

I felt myself relenting. The promise of amazing coffee beans was too enticing to turn down. "Okay, one drink, but never again."

I let him enter first and stuck close behind him to avoid being seen. Although none of my family members would be here, that wouldn't stop the gossip train from running. Every supernatural in town was familiar with the rivalry between my family and Corinne's.

"Oh, wow," I breathed. Magic Beans was much nicer than I anticipated. The interior was stylish and comfortable with upholstered chairs, coffee tables, and garden furniture in pops of color. The counter was in a long L-shape with stools at the short end. A variety of cheerful artwork adorned the butterscotch-colored walls. Although the artistic styles differed from one piece to the next, they somehow worked together as a collection.

Corinne stood proudly behind the counter, overseeing a barista and a cashier. Her looks favored her elegant grandmother, Adele, who served with me on the supernatural council. Corinne's brow lifted a fraction when she saw me approach.

"Welcome to Magic Beans, Eden," Corinne said. "I have to admit, I'm surprised you'd dare to enter."

I leaned forward and lowered my voice. "I'm confident you won't hex my drink."

Corinne smiled. "I'm looking for repeat customers, so that wouldn't exactly be in my best interest, no matter how much my mother would enjoy hearing about it later." Her smile faded. "How do I know you're not here to curse my business?"

"I wouldn't dream of ruining a perfectly good coffee bean," I said. "It would be a crime against nature."

"How do you know mine's any good if you haven't tasted it yet?"

"You can thank my assistant, Neville," I said. "He insists your coffee is on par with the best he's ever tasted."

Neville stepped up to the counter beside me. "It's true. I mean, I have a soft spot for Holes and it's conveniently located next to our office, but I would go out of my way for yours."

Corinne beamed. "What a great compliment. I'll take it." She called over her shoulder. "These two are on the house."

Neville's giddiness was palpable. You'd think she just offered to join his Dungeons & Dragons team.

The barista made coffee drinks with the level of skill Neville used in crafting magical gadgets. I admired my frappe for a full minute before daring to take a sip.

"The verdict?" Neville prompted.

"Liquid heaven."

The shop was so crowded that there were no available tables. It seemed incredible that in a town as small as Chipping Cheddar, I could be in a shop and recognize only a few faces. Then again, I hadn't lived here for years. As much as things seemed the same, they most certainly had changed. Bright hair dye appeared to be in fashion. There were multiple tables with turquoise, fire engine red, and shocking purple heads. Hair dye would have been a welcome form of rebellion in my house. It was my refusal to engage in evil tactics that made me the black—or white—sheep of the family.

"Shall I work a little magic to get a table to open up?" Neville whispered.

"That's okay," I said. "I'll take mine to go. I should head

home and shower anyway." Training made me sweaty and gross.

We turned and headed toward the door.

"Well, well, well. If it isn't the prodigal daughter returned home." Tanner Hughes, my high school boyfriend, intercepted us on our way out. His handsome, chiseled features failed to make up for his repulsive personality, a fact I wished I'd learned before I'd chosen him to be my first.

I sucked down more of my frappe. "Stop pretending you know what prodigal means."

He ignored my jibe. "Is this your new boyfriend?" He gave Neville the once-over. "A little shorter than I'd expect, but I guess a rebound is any port in a storm."

I frowned. "A rebound from what?"

"Chief Fox rejecting your advances. You can hardly blame the guy. He's new in town and even he knows to steer clear of you and your nutty family."

I clenched my hands, fighting the urge to hex him in the middle of the coffee shop. "Chief Fox didn't reject me. We have a professional relationship and that's it."

Tanner took a sip of his coffee. "I heard you've been hounding him so much that he started patrolling with dogs." His lips curved into a cruel smile. "One bitch at a time."

Some people made it *very* difficult to be good.

"Chief Fox is making a community-wide effort to help with dog adoption," Neville said. "And you should watch your tongue when you speak to a federal agent or she may just relieve you of it."

I flashed a bright smile and placed a hand on my hip, as though I had a concealed weapon. Unbeknownst to Tanner, my whole body was a weapon in plain sight.

"If you miss my tongue, Eden, you only have to ask." Tanner winked. "There's no need for violence, although I wouldn't object if you draw a little blood."

I fixed him with a steely gaze. "Neither would I."

Neville muttered an incantation under his breath.

Tanner brought the coffee cup back to his lips for another sip, his smirk still evident. I watched with amusement as the cup tipped too far and the contents spilled all over his white shirt. "What the hell?"

I stroked his arm. "What a pity. Someone's getting clumsy in his old age." I linked my arm through my assistant's. "Come on, Neville. You may be short, but at least you don't need a sippy cup for your coffee."

It was a satisfying exit that made my frappe taste even sweeter.

CHAPTER TWO

I ARRIVED home and said a silent prayer that I could zip straight into the shower without being noticed.

"Eden, is that you?"

I should've known better.

I sauntered into the kitchen, careful to keep my Magic Beans contraband out of view. If I hadn't still been steaming from my run-in with Tanner, I would've remembered to dispose of it before I got home.

"Just got back from training," I said. "I need a quick shower."

My one-year-old nephew Ryan sat in the high chair at the island, shoving blueberries into his purple-stained mouth. My mother, grandmother, and great-aunt sat at the dining table and I noticed a bowl between them filled with herbs.

"What are you up to?" I asked, not bothering to mask my suspicious tone.

"We're making an aphrodisiac to sell down at the senior center," Grandma said.

My eyes bulged. "You're what?"

Grandma cackled. "I figured you'd fall for that. You know,

Eden, if you didn't have a broomstick wedged so firmly up your..."

"Esther," Aunt Thora interrupted, with a quick glance at Ryan.

"What?" Grandma asked. "The kid can't even say his own name yet. I've got months before I need to worry about inappropriate language."

Aunt Thora narrowed her eyes at her sister. "Practice makes perfect."

"Relax, Eden," my mother said primly. "We're not doing anything that would set off your Radar of Good and Evil."

"It's a spell for my lemon trees," Aunt Thora said. "They seem to be under attack."

"Some kind of pest?" I asked.

"Seems to be," Aunt Thora said. "We're creating a protective ward around the trees to keep out any bugs and prevent further damage."

My mother gave me a haughty look. "See? We're helping, not hurting."

"First time for everything," I muttered.

Ryan took a handful of blueberries and chucked them on the floor, laughing maniacally. Three animals came tearing around the corner as though they'd been lying in wait for this very moment.

"Princess Buttercup," I said sternly. My hellhound stopped in her tracks and looked at me with a guilty expression. "No blueberries."

The black cat and the Burmese python had no such compunction and continued full steam ahead. Candy, my grandmother's familiar, decided that she'd rather play with the blueberries than eat them and began to bat them around the floor. Charlemagne's long, slithering body squished as many blueberries as he managed to eat. A trail of purple guts appeared on the kitchen floor.

"Good throw, Ryan," my mother said. "With an arm like that, you'll be casting spells in no time."

I seized this moment of distraction and slipped the empty cup into the trashcan.

"Only if he's a wizard," Aunt Thora said. "It's too soon to tell."

My family seemed more concerned with Ryan's nature than the mess he'd made.

"Ryan, blueberries belong in your mouth, not on the floor," I said. My nephew showed me his gums in response and I wondered whether he was practicing for a lifetime of evil or simply being a toddler. It was hard to tell.

"You should make him sit there until he finds a way to clean the squished ones off the floor," Grandma said. "That'll teach him not to throw food *and* it might trigger his super-natural side. A win-win."

"What if he's a druid like his mother?" my mother asked. "There won't be anything he can do from his high chair."

"That's child abuse," Aunt Thora said. "I'll just use a spell to clean it up."

Grandma blew a raspberry. "That's why Moyer is such a soft touch. You were too easy on him."

Aunt Thora faced her sister. "Are you saying my son is gay because I didn't use excessive force?"

Grandma leaned forward. "I'm saying your son isn't half the demon he might've been because you were too lenient. You used to be fearsome. Motherhood changed you and not for the better."

Aunt Thora bristled. "Moyer is one of the top lawyers in his field. You don't get to the top of that ladder by being too soft."

The room sparked with energy. Definitely my cue to leave. "Time for that shower," I said, and spun on my heel.

"Wait one second, missy. What was that cup you threw in the trash?" my mother asked.

Merciful Hecate. I thought I'd gotten away with it. Slowly, I turned back around. "What cup?"

My mother eyed me. "The one you hid in the trash."

"I didn't hide it," I said. "It's empty. That's what a garbage can is for."

My mother wagged a finger. "I know you, Eden Fury. You're trying to get rid of evidence. It reminds me of that time you stole a jar of my newt eyeballs so you could sell them at school and pretend they were hard candy."

"That wasn't me," I said. "That was Anton."

"A liar *and* a thief." My mother clucked her tongue. "Oh, how the mighty have fallen."

Grandma walked over and popped open the lid of the trashcan. "You've got to be kidding me."

"What?" My mother hurried over to investigate. She gasped at the sight of the cup. "Magic Beans? Eden, have you lost your mind?"

"It's frozen coffee, not cyanide."

She faced me, hands on hips. "I think I would have preferred cyanide to outright treason."

"It's not treason," I said. "You're not the head of state."

My mother's nostrils flared. "I beg to differ."

"She means treachery," Aunt Thora said.

"Yes, that." My mother slammed the lid closed. "I can't believe this. After all we've done for you."

"It's one drink," I said.

"And there are plenty of places to go for that," my mother replied. "Holes. The Daily Grind. Sweet Nyx, I could've made you one here."

"Neville wanted to go after our training session," I said. "I didn't want to be rude."

"So if Neville wants to jump off a bridge, you'd follow?" my mother asked.

"Some leader you are," Grandma said. She looked at my mother. "See what happens when you're too easy on kids? She isn't half the fury she could've been either."

"I blame her father," my mother said. "He let her read too many books at bedtime."

My blood pressure began to rise. "My drink was extraordinary," I practically shouted. "And it was so good that I'll be going back tomorrow."

"Over my dead body," my mother yelled.

"Don't tempt me," I shot back.

I bolted out the back door of the house. My shower would have to wait until the tension had subsided. With the way my mother had looked at me just now, the hot water was guaranteed to turn ice cold—or possibly to tapioca pudding. Wouldn't be the first time.

I decided to seek refuge in my future home and went out to the barn to talk to John, the most normal person within a mile radius. The carpenter was hard at work, hammering a nail into a piece of wood.

"That's quite the sweat you're working up," I said. "And I mean that in a non-sexual way." John and I had briefly tried the dating thing, but decided we were better off as friends.

John stopped hammering and chuckled. "You should've seen your mother out here earlier. As hot as I was, I wanted to wrap myself in a parka and a turtleneck."

"She does possess one of the most penetrating gazes in the history of eyes." She'd used it on Anton and I plenty when we were kids, usually to extract information. *Did your father adhere to the speed limit the entire way to the mall with you kids in the car? Did you eat the last cookie? Did you commit at least one evil act today?* We would squirm and resist, but the gaze always won out.

"How goes the work?" My father's paunchy silhouette appeared between the barn doors.

"Hey, Stan," John said.

I shot the carpenter a quizzical look. "Stan?"

"We're old friends now," my father said. "I come out here as part of my daily walk and we have a nice chat."

I eyed him curiously. "Since when do you take daily walks?"

My father patted his rounded stomach as he joined us inside the barn. "Sally's been pestering me to exercise. She thinks the golf course doesn't count."

"It really doesn't," I said. "You ride in a cart between holes."

"Pffft. Details," my father said.

"What do you two chat about?" I asked. I couldn't imagine what these two had in common to discuss.

"Topics of no interest to you. Golf. Tennis. World Wars."

"Your father's diet." John chuckled. "That tofu recipe was hilarious. I was still laughing about that last night when I ate dinner."

"She's trying to starve me," my father said. "I told her if she wanted to get rid of me that badly, she should just divorce me."

"You complain to John about your wife?"

My father hooked his thumbs through his belt loops. "Both of 'em, actually."

I shook my head. "Sally would be mortified." My mother, too, considering she had the hots for John.

"Everybody needs an outlet," my father said.

"That seems to be your position on a lot of things," I said cryptically. As a vengeance demon, my father took jobs in Otherworld where he was able to use his powers more freely.

"You're right about her posture, though, Stan," John said. "I noticed it when she came in."

My head swung in the carpenter's direction. "Excuse me?"

John made a zigzag motion with the hammer. "Your posture. You should use those core muscles to stand up straight or you could end up with stooped shoulders like some old ladies get."

Anger coiled in my stomach. "Are you seriously criticizing my posture?"

John seemed to realize the error of his ways. "Uh, no. Of course not. What do I know? I'm just a monkey with a hammer."

"Keep it up and you will be," I said.

John laughed, no clue that I could pull that off if I wanted to.

"Dad, you should leave John alone and let him work," I said.

My father walked around the perimeter of the barn, inspecting the work to date. "Same goes for you, Eden. I'm the one paying the bill."

"Half the bill," I said. My mother had agreed to pay the other half.

"Fine," my father said. "So I get to give half an opinion." He fixed his gaze on John. "You're doing excellent work. Keep it up."

"Thank you, sir," John said.

"We'll talk more about Yalta tomorrow when we don't have the Greek chorus over here." My father jabbed a thumb in my direction.

"Can I shower at your house?" I asked, as we exited the barn.

"Why? What'd you do?" My father was intimately familiar with the risks involved in annoying my mother.

"I went to Magic Beans."

He recoiled. "Are you trying to get yourself hexed?"

"I like Corinne."

My father chuckled. "Your mother must've blown a fuse."

We crossed the lawn toward my father's house and I noticed the sickly lemon trees as we passed by. "Any idea what would cause that?"

"I turn a blind eye to most of their projects," my father said.

"Same."

We entered the house through the back door that led straight into the kitchen, where Sally was busy wiping down the countertops. The vampire's OCD tendencies meant that my father's house was always sparkling clean, no magic required.

"Hello, Eden." She stopped wiping and frowned when she noticed my slightly disheveled state. "You've been sweating." Her tone sounded almost accusatory.

"I was training earlier. I need to take a shower in the guest bathroom, if that's okay."

"Of course it's okay," my father interjected.

"What's wrong with your shower?" Sally asked.

"Eden went to Corinne LeRoux's new coffee shop."

Sally's lip curled. "What's one more place for mediocre coffee?" She sighed. "If there's one thing I miss in Other-world, it's the coffee."

"Really?" I perked up. "That's one of things I miss about San Francisco, but I have to say that Magic Beans is really good."

Sally's expression grew dreamy. "Oh, it can't be as good as home. Potis coffee beans are unparalleled."

My father's eyes lit up. "That's the company with the winged monkey logo."

I scrunched my nose. "What does a flying monkey have to do with coffee beans?"

"The CEO is a wicked witch," Sally said. She smiled at her

husband, showing her bright white fangs. "She's just your type, Stanley."

"Not anymore," my father said. "I prefer sanity to wickedness."

"I'll remember you said that the next time you harass me about my fury powers," I said.

"So Eden, what do you think of the neighbor?" Sally asked, smoothly changing the subject before my father and I launched into an argument. She knew us too well.

"What new neighbor?" I asked. "Who moved?"

"For an agent, you sure don't pay much attention," my father said. "It's not like Munster Close is very big."

"Who's the neighbor?" I asked, losing patience.

"His name is Michael Bannon," Sally said. "Human. He moved into Dudley's house after Dudley's family moved him into the nursing home."

"Oh. Is he nice?" I vaguely remembered Dudley. He'd been old even when I was a kid. His house was closer to the mouth of the cul-de-sac.

"He golfs," my father said, his primary concern when it came to humans.

"I'm going to bake him cream cheese muffins," Sally said. "I need a few ingredients from the store first."

"That's kind of you," I said.

"She has ulterior motive," my father said.

Why didn't that surprise me?

"Cheese-chella is coming up and I'm considering entering one of the competitions," Sally said.

I scratched my head. "What's Cheese-chella?"

"FromageFest," my father said.

"Oh, I didn't realize they'd changed the name." The cheese festival is an annual tradition in town that included dozens of vendors' stalls downtown and a flood of tourists. Chipping Cheddar, Maryland was settled by English Puritans, many of whom turned to dairy farming and eventually cheesemaking for their livelihoods, and the street names celebrated this history.

"The town council voted for a new name to make the festival more contemporary," Sally said. "They're trying to appeal to a younger crowd."

"It'll always be FromageFest to me," my father said irritably.

No matter what its name was, I wasn't a fan of the festival for reasons I didn't care to think about. One of the many drawbacks to returning to live in my hometown was a history I couldn't shake.

"Eden, dear, why don't you get that shower now?" Sally suggested. "Your skin looks in need of a good scrub." Sally thought everything looked in need of a good scrub.

"I'm sure you're right," I said. I headed to the guest bathroom, my mind whirring with memories of FromageFest. If only I could scrub away my family's past as easily I could scrub away the dirt.

I heaved a sigh.

If only.

CHAPTER THREE

IN ORDER TO escape my mother's wrath, I made plans to meet up with my best friend, Clara Riley. The more time I spent out of the house, the more likely my mother would have moved on to another perceived injustice when I returned. I hoped.

I pulled into the parking lot of a small yoga and dance studio called Barre None. Clara was convinced that yoga was a critical component missing from my life. Although the gods had blessed me with strength and speed, they were distracted when it came time to hand out flexibility and tranquility.

I'd barely pushed open the door when an eager voice rang out. "Eden Fury, how wonderful to have you home again!"

I peered at the older woman. Her gray hair was pulled back in a tight bun, which only served to accentuate her chipmunk cheeks. She wore a black T-shirt with the words *I Do Yoga Because Punching People Is Frowned Upon* stretched across her ample chest.

"Mrs. Marr?" As the high school principal's secretary, Francine Marr had been a fixture in the office during my years there. If you wanted to be on the principal's good side, it was best to get on Mrs. Marr's good side first.

"That's right, dear. It's been a few years, hasn't it?"

"Are you here for the yoga class?" I asked.

"She teaches it." Clara appeared beside Mrs. Marr in a light pink T-shirt that read *Heavily Meditated*.

"Wow, that's great," I said. "You're not at the high school anymore?"

"I retired, and then quickly realized constant downtime wasn't for me, so I decided to tackle something new," Mrs. Marr said. "Yoga was a revelation for me."

It was heartening to know that, even at Mrs. Marr's age, I could start a new, satisfying chapter in life.

"Eden, you actually came. Color me shocked." Sassafras "Sassy" Persimmons bounced toward me, each step punctuated by the swing of her blond ponytail.

"I didn't realize you'd be here, too, Sassy," I said. The former cheerleader was in a relationship with Tanner, my smarmy ex-boyfriend. In fact, their relationship started in high school, when he and I were still dating, but I digress.

"It's okay, isn't it?" Clara asked quietly. Clara and Sassy's friendship blossomed at *The Buttermilk Bugle*, the town newspaper, where Clara is a fledgling reporter and Sassy sells advertising. Clara and I had been somewhat estranged during my years away. Now that I was back, I'd been trying to accept the presence of Sassy in my life. Some moments were easier than others.

I squeezed Clara's arm to let her feel my emotions and she smiled in response. As an empath, Clara only needed to touch me to know how I felt. Like many gifts, it was both a blessing and a curse. Clara tended to steer clear of romantic relationships because she found the weight of emotions involved too much to bear. I knew she was still struggling to accept the departure of Quinn Redmond, the FBM agent who'd recently come to town to oversee my training. Although they'd fallen hard and fast, his job didn't allow for him to stay in one place very long.

"I'm looking forward to trying this, although—fair warning—I might need to be carried out by paramedics," I said.

Mrs. Marr patted my shoulder. "Not to worry, dear. We accept all kinds here. Beginners have nothing to fear from me."

"Except her peacock pose," Sassy whispered. "It's killer. You should definitely fear that."

Two fit men entered the studio and unrolled their brightly colored mats. One was as toned as the other, although one of them reeked of cologne, which seemed an odd choice for yoga class.

"Shanti, shanti, shanti, girls," the one guy said by way of greeting.

"I don't have a mat," I said, suddenly anxious. I felt as though I'd shown up for a baseball game without a bat and glove.

"Not to worry. I have extras," Mrs. Marr said. She gestured to the far wall where mats were stacked in a neat pile.

"I'll get you one," Sassy offered. She bounced across the room and gave the men a flirtatious smile along the way.

"Sassy still doesn't realize they're married," Clara said.

"Do you really think that would that stop her?" I asked.

Clara smiled. "To each other."

Ah.

"Eden, I'd like you to meet Shayne and Ethan," Mrs. Marr said. "They're two of my dedicated regulars."

Great. More yoga experts to put me to shame. I should have joined my niece's preschool class where I would've been less noticeable.

"Nice to meet you," I said.

"Here you go, Eden." Sassy unrolled a mat for me next to hers. I wasn't sure which placement would be worse—next to the extremely fit guys or the limber former cheerleader.

"Thanks." My gaze was drawn to the logo on Shayne's tank top. "Wow. The Devil's Playground. I haven't thought of that place since I tried to sneak in when Clara and I were in high school."

Clara snorted. "That was not one of our shining moments."

"My brother ratted me out," I said. "I was punished for a week." And by punished, I mean they put a protective ward around the house that prevented me from leaving except for going to and from school. If I tried to leave at an unauthorized time, I got zapped. Painfully.

Shayne winked at me. "Ethan owns the place. That's how we met."

My gaze flickered to Shayne's husband. "Do you? How cool. I always wanted to see the inside."

"Well, you're old enough now," Ethan said. "We've got a fantastic band lined up for tomorrow night. You should come by."

"Maybe I will," I said, assuming I was able to function for the next couple of days after this class. No promises.

"I've never heard of it," Sassy said, appearing confused. "How can you all know about a bar I've never heard of?"

"It's not your kind of crowd," Clara said.

Sassy's brow lifted. "Oh," she whispered. "It's one of those darkly lit bars for unattractive people?"

"Yes, exactly," I said firmly. That would end Sassy's interest right there.

Sassy swung the end of her ponytail over her shoulder. "That's fine. I have plans tomorrow night. I'm helping Bridget McKay practice for the Miss Chipping Cheddar parade. I'm sure you remember that *I* wore the crown when we were fifteen."

I tensed at the mention of the festival. Maybe no one here would remember.

"I'm teaching Bridget how to walk and smile," Sassy said.

I gave a mock gasp. "At the same time?"

Sassy climbed onto her mat on all fours and arched her back. "You're just upset because your family's banned from attending."

So much for no one remembering.

Shayne gave me a curious look. "Your family is banned from Cheese-chella?"

"All of them," Sassy replied for me. She seemed annoyingly satisfied to tell the story. "They caused chaos the year I was Miss Chipping Cheddar. Several stalls were ruined. It was a miracle no one was hurt."

"Sassy," Clara said softly.

Ethan and Shayne stared at me, clearly eager to hear the rest of the story.

"Oh, I remember that year," Mrs. Marr said. "Such excitement. Seeing the firemen in action was a real highlight." She took her place at the front of the room and sat cross-legged on her mat. "I'd forgotten it was your family, Eden."

"It was an accident," Clara said. "The story was completely exaggerated."

I smiled gratefully. Clara had earned her best friend stripes with unfailing loyalty and a non-judgmental approach to my family.

"Tanner's mom saw the whole thing," Sassy said. "She said that Eden's grandmother tried to set fire to Eden's mom, and one of the stalls caught fire, which then spread to the entire row."

"I never believed it," Mrs. Marr said. "What kind of woman tries to set fire to her own daughter?"

The kind that's dipped in evil water at birth, I wanted to reply, but held my tongue.

"Eden's grandmother used to smoke," Clara said. "She accidentally set fire to a stall when she was lighting a cigarette. The crisis was averted."

That was partially true. Grandma had been a heavy smoker for years until my mother threatened to kick her out of the house if she didn't quit. They'd been fighting about it in the middle of the festival and had nearly come to blows. My mother had tried to relieve Grandma of her cigarettes and lighter and naturally magic came into play. I stupidly tried to intervene by siphoning magic from both witches in an effort to subdue them. Needless to say, it didn't go well for anyone. Aunt Thora was able to douse most of the flames before the firefighters arrived. Still, most of my family was banned from future festivals as a result.

"Why don't we focus on more pleasant thoughts?" Mrs. Marr suggested. "Presumably, Eden is here to relax and clear her mind, not clutter it with painful memories."

"Thank you," I said.

"On that note, why don't we start with a few minutes of silence in order to transition into the present?" Mrs. Marr said. She tapped the screen of her phone and the soothing sounds of the ocean began to play. "We'll start in corpse pose."

I flinched. "Did you say corpse?"

"Savasana is the pose of complete relaxation," Mrs. Marr said.

I watched Clara move onto her back with her arms and legs at forty-five degree angles. Unsurprisingly, Sassy paused to admire her own form in the mirror on the wall before assuming the position. The soft curve of her lips told me the reflection met with her approval.

The moment I closed my eyes and tried to relax, I started

to doze off. When I realized I was falling asleep, my whole body jerked upward and I yelled out, "No, Fergus!"

Sassy snickered. "Who's Fergus? Your boyfriend in San Francisco?"

"My old FBI partner," I said, my cheeks warm from embarrassment.

"You were an FBI agent?" Ethan asked, turning his head toward me while in corpse position.

"I still am," I said. It was a necessary lie. "I work out of a small satellite office."

Shayne and Ethan exchanged glances. "Here in Chipping Cheddar?" Shayne asked. "We don't even warrant a Starbucks, yet we have an FBI office?"

"Don't need a Starbucks," I said. "The Daily Grind is excellent and Magic Beans is my new favorite."

"I haven't tried Magic Beans yet," Ethan said, "though I adore Rosalie LeRoux, so I would definitely like to support her daughter."

"How do you know Rosalie?" I asked.

"She read palms at our wedding," Shayne said.

Of course she did.

Mrs. Marr snapped her fingers. "We're supposed to be in the pose of the dead. That means silence. Remember, the dead don't speak."

"Ha!" I said. Try telling that to Alice Wentworth or some of the other ghosts I'd encountered.

"What was that, Eden?" Mrs. Marr said.

"Nothing," I mumbled.

"Now we're going to move into paschimottanasana," Mrs. Marr said. How she managed to get her body that flat, I had no idea.

"What do you think?" Clara asked me. "Ready to try this one?"

"I can't even pronounce it, let alone try it," I said.

"It's easy," Sassy proclaimed.

So are you, I wanted to say, but refrained for Clara's sake.

The next pose was equally challenging. I glanced next to me to see Sassy in a position that I'd inadvertently witnessed when I caught Anton watching porn when we were younger.

"I'm starting to understand what Tanner sees in you," I said.

"Your issue isn't with your flexibility," Mrs. Marr said. "It's your inability to relax."

"What? I'm relaxed," I said. I jiggled my arms to show how limp they were for good measure.

"You seem as relaxed as a vampire in church," Mrs. Marr said.

My shoulders stiffened all over again. "Excuse me?"

The older woman laughed. "It's just an expression, dear. I didn't want to shame women by using the whore-in-church analogy."

"And whores everywhere thank you for that," I said, "including the one in here."

Sassy narrowed her eyes at me.

"Let's slowly rise and move into tree pose," Mrs. Marr said. She stood with her hands pressed together above her head and a foot pressed against the inside of her opposite leg.

I copied her pose with relative ease this time.

"Oh my, I…I feel dizzy," Mrs. Marr said. Before anyone could intervene, the older woman toppled over.

"Francine," Ethan said. He scrambled from his mat and was the first to reach her.

"Maybe her bun was too tight and it cut off her circulation," Sassy said.

I cut her a sharp glance. Every time I wanted to view Sassy in a new light, she reminded me that it would be an uphill battle.

Mrs. Marr moaned and opened her eyes. "That was unpleasant," she whispered, still flat on the mat.

"Did you lose your balance?" Shayne asked.

"No, she was practicing a new position called Gravity Wins," I said. As soon as the sarcasm rolled of my tongue, I wished I could snatch it back. It was hard to overcome a lifetime of conditioning.

"At least the mat cushioned her fall," Sassy said.

"The mat?" Mrs. Marr murmured. "It was my extra layer of blubber." She moved to a seated position and put her head between her legs. "It's finally good for something, so I'm giving it credit."

Clara brought her a water bottle. "How do you feel now?"

Mrs. Marr touched her head. "That's never happened to me before. I think I might be coming down with something."

"My bartender called out sick last night," Ethan said. "I think something's going around."

"I felt woozy before I left the house," Mrs. Marr admitted. "I thought my seasonal allergies were flaring up."

"It still might be that," Clara said. "But you should hydrate and rest."

Mrs. Marr nodded. "I'm sorry about class, everyone. I'll refund you."

"Don't worry about that," Ethan said. "You focus on your health."

Shayne and Ethan offered to drive Mrs. Marr home and she gratefully accepted.

"Well, your first yoga class was certainly exciting," Clara said, as we exited the building.

"It's not supposed to be," Sassy said. "That's the whole point. It's Nama-stay awake but in a calm and collected state."

I moved my neck from side to side. "I feel more flexible already."

Clara gave me a critical look. "You're just saying that."

"Of course I am, but mind over matter, right?"

Clara bit back a smile. "You just think if you say it often enough, your body would eventually believe it."

I gave her arm a playful punch. "I think I liked it better when we weren't speaking."

Sassy sucked in a breath. "Whoa, that's dark."

Clara's expression crumpled. "Don't even joke. Let's never do that again."

"You're right. I'm sorry." I paused.

"I'll see you at the office, Clara," Sassy said. "I have a client meeting in an hour."

I waited until Sassy was out of earshot to ask, "Have you heard from Agent Redmond?"

Clara's eyes brimmed with unshed tears. "We decided it was best to…" She cut herself off, unable to continue.

"I'm going to stop now, before I say something catastrophic," I said. "How about coming to The Devil's Playground tonight? That sounds fun."

She shook her head. "Too many bodies knocking into me means too many emotions."

"I'm clearly the worst friend ever. Are you sure you want to stay friends with me?"

Clara wrapped her arms around me and gave me a tight squeeze. "Always."

CHAPTER FOUR

"ARE you sure you're going out?" my mother asked.

"What kind of question is that?" I asked. "Who else would be sure if not me? I'm the one doing it."

My mother's critical gaze traveled from my head to my feet. "Okay, if you say so."

I groaned. "What's the problem?"

"There's no problem," she replied. "I know you're not one for keeping up appearances. You be you, sweetheart." She pinched my cheek.

I glanced down at my light gray capris and a black sleeveless top. "What's wrong with me?"

My mother took a step back, assessing me fully. "Where do I start? I was going to lead with your shoes, but we can discuss your hair first."

I closed my eyes in an effort not to roll them. It didn't work. Turns out they roll just as well when the lids are closed.

"I brushed my hair and used the straightener to defrizz it," I said. "What more do you want from me?"

"It's nothing *I* want from you, honey, but if you want *men* to want something from you, you're going to have to do a little better than that."

"I'm going to listen to a band in a dark bar," I said. "My hair and clothes will be mere silhouettes."

"No one notices a silhouette unless it's built like Jessica Rabbit," my mother said.

"What's this about rabbits?" Grandma entered the kitchen in her robe and bunny slippers.

"A little early for that ensemble, isn't it?" I asked.

"I'm old," Grandma said. "You think I register time like a normal being?"

"I don't think you register emotions like a normal being," I muttered.

My mother folded her arms. "I find it fascinating that you make a stink when I mention your outfit, yet you have no trouble commenting on Grandma's."

"That's not an outfit," I said.

My mother nodded firmly. "My opinion exactly."

I retrieved my purse from the counter. "I'm going out. Don't wait up."

Footsteps thundered down the steps. "Wait! I'll go with you." My brother appeared at the entrance to the kitchen, nearly breathless.

"What's going on?" I asked.

"Nothing," he said quickly. "We're going now, right?"

"Anton," Verity yelled. "You come back here this instant. I need help."

"Code Five," Anton said, his hair disheveled and his eyes wild.

My brow creased. "What's a Code Five?"

My mother blanched. "Which one?"

"Ryan," he said.

"Which end?" Grandma added.

Anton fought for breath. "The bottom half."

My mother grimaced. "Oh no, diapers. At least Olivia is able to use the toilet."

I didn't need to hear anymore. "Let's go."

"I'll light the charmed candles," Aunt Thora said from her place at the table. "They'll absorb the smell."

"Call your father and tell him it's his turn to babysit," my mother said.

"Sorry, Mom," Anton said. "It's every man for himself."

Anton and I bolted outside just as a vile stench overtook the house.

"You're driving," I said.

Anton patted the keys in his pocket. "Gladly. Which bar?"

We hopped in his Audi and I immediately buckled up, remembering my brother's driving skills.

"The Devil's Playground," I said. "I've never been and there's supposedly a good band playing tonight."

He started to laugh. "Remember that time…"

I gave a solemn shake of my head. "No need to make me relive it."

"I owe you one," Anton said. "Ryan's a mess right now. I thought it was only a cold, but it seems to have morphed into something worse."

"And you left your wife holding the diaper bag?" I clucked my tongue. "She's not a druid. She's a saint."

The Devil's Playground is nestled in the woods on the outskirts of town. Its remote location makes it less likely for unsuspecting humans to wander in.

Anton pulled into the dirt parking lot and squeezed between two pickup trucks. "Tuck the side mirror in so no one knocks into it," he said.

We studied the exterior of the building, hunting for the entrance. "They sure don't roll out the red carpet for customers, do they?" my brother said.

"It's supposed to be secret, like a speakeasy during Prohibition."

"That only works in an alleyway where everyone walks," Anton said. "This packed parking lot is kind of a dead giveaway that the building isn't abandoned."

"You can take that up with Ethan," I said. "He's the owner." I was curious to talk more to Ethan.

"It's smart business to cater to supernaturals here, although I preferred human bars when I was still in that phase," Anton said.

I lifted an eyebrow. "You think you're out of the bar phase? Did I blink and miss it?"

He shrugged. "A wife. A career. Two young kids. A side gig. Yeah, I'm not exactly swimming in ale these days."

"Well, here's your big chance to enjoy a night out," I said. "Consider it my gift to you."

We pressed a hidden button that took us more time to find than I was willing to admit and the door slid aside. A bouncer stood sentry inside, waiting to check our IDs. Two members of the band were setting up their instruments on the stage. The banner pinned on the wall behind them read *Ghost of Billy Crystal*.

"That's macabre," I said. "Billy Crystal's not even dead, is he?"

Anton pulled out his phone and Googled. "Nope. Great shape, too."

Phew. Robin Williams had been hard enough to accept. I couldn't handle Billy Crystal, too.

A familiar blast of cologne forced a cough from my lungs.

"You made it. Fantastic!" Shayne said. Ethan's husband looked dapper in smart black trousers and a crimson shirt.

"Hi, Shayne. This is my brother, Anton," I said.

"Great to meet you," Shayne said.

"Oh, there's Ethan," I said.

The owner emerged from a back room, trailed by two more bandmates—a man and a woman. Both of their noses were bright red and a stash of tissues peeked out of the guy's pockets. They continued to the stage and Ethan broke away to greet us.

"Hey, Eden. Congratulations. You can finally mark this place off your bucket list," Ethan said.

"No chance of punishment tonight," I said. "My family was happy to get rid of me. This is Anton, my brother."

Ethan scrutinized him. "Do I detect a hint of vengeance demon?"

"I tend to be non-practicing, for the most part."

"I know how you feel," Ethan said. "I'm a selkie, but I spend far more time on land than in water."

"You're human with the Sight?" I asked Shayne.

He nodded. "I'm also a scuba diver, so we can pretty much spend time anywhere together."

Ethan gave me an appraising look. "I know you're one of us, but I can't for the life of me figure out what you are."

"You have a strange black aura," Shayne said.

"That's just my shadow," I joked. I wanted to avoid any discussion of my true nature.

"She's a fury," Anton announced proudly. "Her powers are terrifying."

I closed my eyes and mentally counted to ten. "Thanks, big brother."

"Show them your wings," Anton urged.

"I am not showing my wings in a crowded bar," I said through gritted teeth.

"You have wings?" Ethan asked, intrigued.

"I cloak them," I said. "It's not like I need them in the modern world. The gods haven't quite caught up to airplanes."

"Check out her eyes," Anton continued. "They've got these cool little flames in them now."

Ethan and Shayne both leaned forward to gaze into my eyes. "What does that mean?" Shayne asked. He was so close that I nearly gagged on his cologne.

"Means she's immortal," Anton said.

Ethan observed me closely. "You're not really FBI, are you?"

"I was, before I moved back home." Probably best to avoid the circumstances that brought me here. Fergus's near-death experience was an accident and one that I vowed never to repeat.

"Now she's FBM," Anton said. "She took over for Paul Pidcock."

Ethan snapped his fingers. "Right. I heard about that whole thing. I didn't realize you took over for him."

"Nice guy," Shayne added. "He used to come in here on occasion, if he needed information from Ethan."

Not a bad idea. I'd add it to my mental list.

I shifted my attention to the stage where the band was warming up. "What about the entertainment? I'm getting a mixed vibe."

"Three supers," Ethan said. "The lead singer is human, though."

"Sighted?" I asked.

Ethan shook his head. "Not this one. He has no clue that his bandmates have more fur than Cruella De Vil."

"Are they any good?" I asked. "I've never heard their music before."

"And you might not tonight either," Ethan said. "The drummer and the lead singer both have colds and the singer's worried about going hoarse during the performance."

"I'd rather be immune than immortal," I said.

"That's because you're a baby when you're sick," Anton said.

I gave my brother a pointed look. "Says the guy that abandoned his own baby over a Code Five."

Anton bristled. "I left him in his mother's capable hands. She's a healer, which makes her the best parent for the job."

The band began to play and, while the music itself was good, I had a feeling the singer's scratchy voice wasn't intentional.

"If you'll excuse us," Ethan said. "Time to make the rounds."

As Anton and I bobbed our heads to the music, I felt a pair of eyes on me from across the room. I craned my neck to see a scruffy guy in a white muscle shirt eyeing me from the bar. Terrific. He treated eye contact as an invitation and sauntered toward me. The muscle shirt was a bad choice for many reasons, but mainly because his body was so scrawny that I was pretty sure I could blow him backward with a deep sigh.

He sidled up to me, his beady eyes dancing with interest. "Hey there. Name's Chris. Your scent attracted me from across the room and I just had to come over and introduce myself."

Only a werewolf would lead with a line like that. "I'm not really interested in making new friends tonight, Chris, but thanks."

He leaned closer and sniffed me. "Are you sure about that? You smell awfully friendly to me."

Beside me, Anton twitched and I placed a steadying hand on his arm. I didn't need my big brother to protect me from creeps. I had years of experience.

I fully faced the werewolf. "And you smell like you bathed in wet leaves and then dried off with bark."

The werewolf seemed to take the insult as a compliment.

"Nature's perfume," he said. "Are you new in town? I come here a lot, but I don't recognize you."

"My name is Eden," I said. "My cousins are werewolves. You must know Julie and Meg."

He frowned. "You're Julie's cousin?"

"Rafael, technically," I said. "Julie's husband."

Chris's head snapped back. "The wizard?"

"And amazing chef," I added.

Chris backed away slightly. "You're Eden Fury." He flashed a nervous smile. "You know what? I see an old friend by the bar. Nice to meet you." He practically left scorch marks on the floor.

I turned to smile at my brother. "I guess he's heard of our family."

Anton gaped at me. "Is this what it's like for you? No wonder you don't date."

"I still don't know how you managed to convince someone as wonderful as Verity to take a chance on you."

Anton rocked back on his heels. "I am a lucky demon."

"Make sure you tell her that when you get home."

The drummer sneezed and one of the drumsticks slipped from her hand and shot into the crowd. Someone gave a triumphant scream and held up the stick. I'm not sure she realized it was an accident. The drummer carried on in vain with a single drumstick.

"This poor band," I said. The singer's voice seemed to worsen by the minute.

"Can't you do a spell to help them?" Anton asked.

"You know I don't use magic frivolously."

Anton grunted. "Sometimes I wish you were more like Mom."

I recoiled. "What did you just say?"

"The drummer lost her stick," he said. "What's the big

deal? You have so much angst over Mom being evil, but not using your magic for someone in need is the real injustice."

"I don't think I need advice on justice from a vengeance demon, but thanks," I said.

"Why not? We have the best vantage point."

Someone chucked the missing drumstick back to the stage and the drummer caught it with her free hand.

"See?" I said. "It all worked out. No magic required."

"You're just saying that to make yourself feel better for being a magic hoarder."

I was starting to regret bringing my brother along. "I am *not* a hoarder."

"You might as well get involved with Chief Fox because it's not like you act like a supernatural anyway. Just be a human and go make human babies with the law-enforcing underwear model."

I hugged myself. "I wouldn't make human babies, Anton. That's part of the problem. Chief Fox would have no idea what he'd signed up for. It isn't fair."

"Then tell him. He's a grown man. Let him decide."

I choked. "Have you lost your mind? Are you seriously suggesting that I reveal to the chief of police that there's a supernatural world and I'm from a long line of evil-doers?"

Anton shrugged. "You never know. He might be cool with it."

I started to laugh. "You're living in a fantasy land, brother."

There was a brief lull as the band began its next song. At this point, the singer's voice was too strained to understand and the drummer's sneezes seemed more like a strange attempt at harmonizing.

Shayne stepped into the empty space beside me. "They're usually better than this," he said.

I arched an eyebrow. "You think?"

"Ethan should've canceled them," Shayne said. "Ray sounds like he swallowed an entire litter of kittens and that drummer has sneezed so many times, I'm pretty sure we'll all leave here with a parting gift."

I shuddered at the thought. Good thing Sally wasn't here. If only my stepmom still had a beating heart, she'd have a coronary over the spreading germs.

"Do you have any magic-infused alcohol that might strengthen everyone's natural defenses?" I asked.

Shayne lit up. "Spoken like a true witch. I'll talk to the bartender right now."

"I'm not a witch…" I began, but he was already gone.

"You don't have to make such an effort to distance yourself," Anton said. "Fury. Witch. It's all the same to someone like Shayne."

"You know I don't want to be associated with them," I said.

Anton mimicked me. "Wah. Wah. My name is Eden and I'm so tortured." He inclined his head. "Are you sure you're not part vampire? Because you sure whine like one."

I folded my arms in a huff and faced the stage. Now I *really* regretted bringing my brother. This was supposed to be a fun night out and instead I was getting doused in germs and insulted by family. I could've stayed home for that.

The singer wobbled toward the microphone and a hacking cough reverberated from the sound system. He gripped the pole to steady himself and tried to resume singing, but it was no use. He couldn't seem to form words. The bass player sensed trouble and picked up the vocals where the lead singer left off.

"He looks like he's trying to do the DUI walk," Anton said, as the lead singer staggered forward in a daze. He reached the edge of the stage and tipped forward. The crowd cheered, thinking he wanted to body surf. They passed him from one pair of hands to the next, the singer's body still and sagging.

"Anton," I said in a quiet voice. "His eyes are open."

"I guess he likes to see his admirers up close," Anton said.

"No," I said. "I don't mean that kind of open. He's not blinking." I watched as the singer was passed to the fringe of the crowd.

"He has to be blinking, Eden. If he's not blinking, he's…"

Someone in the crowd screamed.

"Dead," a woman shrieked. "He's dead."

I turned and faced my brother. "That."

CHAPTER FIVE

THE BAR WAS MOSTLY CLEARED out by the time Chief Fox arrived. Ethan didn't want too many supernaturals lurking in one place when law enforcement showed up, not that the chief would know any better. We all looked human to him.

Anton and I remained in the background while the body was prepared for transport to the Chief Medical Examiner's Office. Ethan joined us after speaking with Chief Fox.

"What was the singer's name?" I asked.

"Ray Langdon," Ethan said. "He was only twenty-eight."

Too young to die of natural causes, unless he had an underlying condition that weakened his immune system.

"Should I hang around?" Anton asked. I knew what he was really asking—did I want to be alone with the chief?

"I'm only here for official reasons," I said. I wanted to be able to brief the chief on the singer's behavior leading up to his unfortunate demise.

"I think I'll go anyway," Anton said. "That way he can give you a ride in his squad car." He wiggled his eyebrows suggestively.

"How do you manage to make even the most innocuous sentences sound dirty?"

Anton buffed his nails on his shirt. "Everyone thinks it's vengeance, but that's my real talent."

"What's your real talent?" Chief Fox's voice pierced the quiet.

"Timing," Anton replied. He shook the chief's hand. "Good to see you again. Don't work too late." My brother left the bar without a backward glance.

"Good evening, Chief," I said.

"More like good morning, but sure," he said.

"Were you asleep?" I asked.

He stifled a yawn. "Doesn't matter now. Duty calls, so I'm here."

"You look tired," I said.

"You would be too if a little pug kept pestering you to go out and pee every five minutes." He managed a smile. "Not that I blame him. He loves the grass. You should see him roll around on his back."

"I can imagine." Princess Buttercup preferred to scorch the grass with her fiery saliva, but the pug thing sounded cute. "Are you crating him at night?"

"I was," he said, "but then I accidentally fell asleep with him in the bed and he snuggled on the pillow next to me." He shook his head. "Agent Fury, you've never seen anything so adorable in your whole life. I couldn't bear to put him back in the crate after that."

I couldn't blame him. I had a hard time saying no to Princess Buttercup, too. One look into those soulful eyes and I melted like butter in the microwave.

"So care to tell me what happened here tonight?" Chief Fox asked, switching deftly to professional mode.

I explained about the band members with colds and the

lead singer hacking up a lung before literally falling to his death.

"Hmm." The chief stroked his dimpled chin and I longed to swat his hand away and replace it with my lips. "Maybe drugs involved, although Ethan over there insists the band is all about clean living. Wheatgrass shots. That sort of thing. I'll order a tox screen to be on the safe side."

"He didn't drink anything except water tonight because he felt too sick," I said. "It could even be an overdose of cold medicine. I've read about cases like that."

"I'll need to get a hold of his medical records. Make sure there wasn't something else going on that nobody knew about." He stared at the place on the floor where the body had been. "There does seem to be something going around. My dentist cancelled on me this morning because he'd come down with something."

Ethan joined our conversation. "You won't need to close the bar, will you?"

"When do you normally reopen?" the chief asked.

"Tomorrow night at ten," Ethan said.

"I'll have a look around now," the chief said. "Depending on what I find, health and safety might have to come in."

Ethan's expression soured. "I understand. I'll go finish up in the office."

"I can help you while I'm here," I said to the chief. "You'll finish faster."

The chief wore a vague smile. "I'll bet."

I swatted his arm. "Mind out of the gutter."

He grinned. "Sorry. Couldn't resist." He walked toward the stage and surveyed the area. "Meet anyone interesting here tonight?"

"Didn't want to," I said. "I only came to get out of the house. My family was driving me nuts."

"Must be hard living home again after years away," he

said. "I can't imagine how I would do in my parents' house in Iowa. I'd probably resort to being their son again, instead of a grown man, if you know what I mean."

"Oh, I do. My family acts like I'm frozen in time. There are some evenings I expect them to ask me if I finished my homework."

The chief crouched over a discarded tissue. "I know it's not your area, but I'll let you know when I get the autopsy report, if you're interested."

I wish I could let him know exactly how interested I really was. "Thanks," I said instead. "I'm happy to help however I can."

We finished our search of the bar and left the building with Ethan so he could lock up.

"Please let me know what you find out, Chief," Ethan said.

The chief gave a crisp nod. "I will."

Ethan strode toward his open-top jeep and climbed in.

"Would you mind giving me a lift home?" I asked. "Anton left with the car."

"I'd be happy to," the chief said.

We walked to his car in comfortable silence. There was something oddly soothing about his presence, despite the nuclear-level sexual tension between us.

He opened the passenger door and I slid into the seat, my heart thumping hard. The slutty part of me wanted to straddle him right here in the dark parking lot—my mother's DNA shining through. I immediately rolled down the window to let in the cool breeze. Close proximity to the chief made me warm all over, so the night air was both delightful and necessary.

"You okay?" he asked, casting a sidelong glance at me as he pulled onto the road.

"Just hot," I said. I fanned myself and turned toward the

open window but not before catching the slightest hint of a smile on his handsome face.

"Are you sure you want to go straight home?" he asked.

I didn't dare look at him and risk letting him see my flushed cheeks. "Where would we go?"

"I'm fully awake now. Might as well take the scenic route home."

I rolled the window halfway up so I could better hear him. "Have you ever seen the town from the lighthouse at night? It's very pretty."

"Won't Mr. O'Neill be there?" he asked.

"He doesn't live there," I said, although it seemed like it. "He definitely won't be there at this hour."

"I wouldn't mind seeing the view," the chief said, "although the one right here is pretty good, too."

The chief looked like an underwear model in uniform, but he thought the view in *my* direction was good? I had to remind myself that he didn't know about my family's nature or our history. He wasn't scared off like Chris the werewolf because he didn't know any better. He thought I was like him —a member of law enforcement. A human. I had to keep it that way.

"*Just* the view," I said.

He grinned. "I can live with that."

I pretended to find a hidden key in a slot in the side of the lighthouse and used a gentle puff of magic to open the lock. A basic spell like this would barely register on the magic scale.

Our climb to the top of the lighthouse became a competition, with the chief determined to stay at least one set ahead of me. I couldn't tell him that it wasn't a fair fight. That I could use my speed or even my wings to beat him to the top. Not that I would.

"You're not even out of breath," he said, when we reached the top.

"I do a lot of physical training," I said.

"Seems a waste for a cybercrime agent," Chief Fox said.

I crossed the round room for a full view of the bay. The stars reflected in the dark water, and it seemed as though the entire world was speckled with diamonds.

"Clear nights are the best," I said. I felt his presence next to me and began to regret my decision to come here. It was too romantic. I should've asked him to drive me straight home.

"We don't have any views like this in Iowa," he said. "I mean, I have a soft spot for Okoboji…"

"Okoboji?" I asked. "Sounds like something out of Star Wars."

He chuckled. "I have many fond memories on that lake, I'll have you know."

"Before the Stormtroopers invaded?"

He cocked his head, analyzing me. "You'd look pretty good with two buns on the side of your head." He reached for my hair and gently twisted long strands around his hands. "Better than good, in fact." He let go of my hair and took a moment to admire my face. "Your eyes. I've never seen anything like them. I see flames."

They were fiery and full of need. That's what he saw. And maybe a little trace of immortality.

"It's a birthmark," I lied.

"In both eyes? How extraordinary." He swept a stray hair off my face. "Not that it surprises me. You're a pretty extraordinary woman, Eden Fury."

My pulse sped up. "You should really stop complimenting me now."

He edged closer. "Why? What will happen?"

"Nothing," I said, splaying my hands against his firm chest. "Because nothing is all that can happen."

He placed a hand over mine. "You feel that, don't you?"

"My heartbeat?" I was pretty sure everyone in town could feel the small earthquake.

"No, the connection," he said. "I don't know what it is about you, but there's something there. Something I've never felt before."

My thoughts grew fuzzy as he pressed closer. "I know. I feel the same." What if we just indulged ourselves this one time? A one-night stand wouldn't endanger him.

"Eden, I won't push you."

I leaned forward, my lips hovering dangerously close to his. The reality was that it would never be just one time with us. Neither one of us seemed partial to one-night stands and I didn't want to sleep with him and then cut him off. That would hurt our professional relationship.

Ugh. For once in my life I hated being good.

"It's not that I'm not interested," I blurted. I took a huge step backward. "There's an FBI rule. It's protocol."

His brow lifted. "Is that so?"

"Neville was reviewing the rules and regulations with me after Agent Redmond left and I saw it then."

He scratched the back of his neck. "I didn't realize...I guess it makes sense. I guess I never had a reason to care one way or another."

"I can't break the rules, Chief. I don't want to jeopardize either of our jobs."

He rubbed my biceps. "No, we're both new to our roles here. It wouldn't be good for our careers."

"I'm sorry," I said.

"Not half as sorry as I am." He pressed his forehead against mine. "If you don't mind, I think I'd better drive you home now."

CHAPTER SIX

Voices drew me downstairs the next morning earlier than I would've preferred after my late night with the chief. I nearly tripped on Charlemagne on my way down the attic steps. The python had decided it would be fun to wrap himself around each step in a loop, creating a series of knots in his body.

"Why would you do this to yourself?" I asked, when I reached his head at the bottom.

Verity rounded the corner in pajamas, her face pinched in annoyance. "There you are, Charlemagne. Where is it?"

"Where's what?" I asked.

"He ran off with Ryan's Slinky," Verity said. "Ryan's cranky enough when he's sick. I don't need him upset, too." She bent over the snake, hands on hips. "How do you propose to get yourself out of this one?"

"I can unknot him from the tail end," I said. "Unloop each section."

Verity wagged a finger at the python. "Aren't you lucky to have Eden here? I would've left you to figure it out on your own."

Charlemagne's tongue darted out and I stroked his head. "I'll handle it. You get ready for work."

Verity's expression softened. "Thanks, Eden."

I knew it was challenging for her, working as a doctor in town and raising two young children. It didn't help that my brother didn't pitch in as much as he should.

"You're not worried, are you?" I asked.

"About Charlemagne? I don't think he actually ate the Slinky."

"No, I mean Ryan," I said. "Whatever's going around…"

Verity squeezed my shoulder. "I already drew a blood sample. I'll get the results later today."

"What are you looking for?" I asked.

"Don't know," she said. "Could be completely unrelated. Could be a standard infection making the rounds and that singer got unlucky." She managed a small smile. "I'm sure you would agree that information is power."

"Always."

Verity returned to her room and I liberated Charlemagne from the steps so that he could resume his reign of terror on the toys.

"Eden, is that you?" a deep voice called.

I entered the kitchen to see Uncle Moyer and his husband, Tomas. My family had been surprised by Uncle Moyer's choice of an angel-human hybrid husband, but Tomas's laid-back attitude and penchant for excessive compliments eventually won everyone over.

"I thought I heard a distinctly masculine voice," I said. "I assumed it was Grandma."

"Eden, you gorgeous magical creature." Tomas vacated his spot at the table to greet me with an airy kiss on each cheek.

"I didn't know you two were coming for breakfast or I would've at least brushed my teeth," I said.

"It wasn't planned," Tomas said, "but nobody makes a

better breakfast than my mother-in-law. If that's black magic at work, then lock me out of paradise right now."

"Knowing you, you're already locked out because you lost your key," Grandma said.

Tomas raked a hand through his unkempt blond hair. "That's why I married Mr. Responsibility, so that I don't have to keep track of such things."

"And here I thought it was my keen intellect and my dashing good looks that sucked you in," Uncle Moyer said.

I noticed a glistening transparent shield around my nephew. "Who put Ryan in a bubble?" I asked.

"It was my request," Uncle Moyer said. "I have an appointment with a very important client this morning and I couldn't take the risk."

Ryan seemed oblivious to the protective bubble and happily tossed oatmeal and banana slices around the tray of his high chair.

"Is there any oatmeal left for me?" I asked.

Aunt Thora gestured to a bowl on the counter. "Still hot, too."

"Thank you." I added honey and cinnamon and stood at the island to eat. "Where's Mom?"

As if on cue, my mother sashayed into the kitchen, still in her pink silk robe with an eye mask pushed to the top of her head. Her eyes and cheeks were puffy and her nose was red and seemingly itchy from the way she kept scratching it.

"The end is nigh," my mother said. "I have the dreaded lurgy."

Verity entered the kitchen behind my mother, now fully dressed. "What are your symptoms, other than the ones I can see?"

Grandma smothered her response with a cough. "Man flu."

My mother's eyes narrowed, which basically eliminated them all together because they were so swollen.

"You don't look on the verge of expiring," I said.

My mother put a hand on her hip. "Oh, look who's an expert now that she's immoral."

"You mean immortal," I said.

Uncle Moyer snapped to attention. "You're immortal now? When did that happen?"

"Nobody tells us anything," Tomas complained.

"I'm sorry," I said. "Next time I'll have announcements printed up."

"You could at least have made a vague Facebook post," Uncle Moyer said. "I would've figured it out."

"That would require me to have a Facebook account," I said.

Verity scrutinized my mother. "Stick out your tongue." My mother complied. "Any digestive issues?"

"Not yet, but I expect I'll have it much worse than Ryan," my mother said.

"Why?" Verity asked.

"Well, because it's me," my mother said. "I do everything better, even illnesses."

"You'll be fine." Verity padded over to the counter for coffee.

"You don't sound concerned," my mother said.

"Are you complaining or relieved?" Grandma asked from the table.

"There's only been one death," Verity said. "It's sad, but these things happen. The flu kills thousands each year, but we don't start building bunkers at the beginning of flu season. We take precautions and go about our lives."

"That's a sensible attitude, Verity," Aunt Thora said.

"Would someone mind removing the bubble from my son so I can finish feeding him?" Verity asked.

Uncle Moyer scooted his chair away and Verity took her place next to Ryan as the bubble dissipated.

My mother ripped off her eye mask and tossed it onto the counter in a dramatic fashion. "Who cares for sensible when I'm on the threshold of death?"

"Does that mean you're at death's door or you've only made it to the front porch?" Grandma asked.

My mother ignored her. "What should I do, Verity? Do you have any potions to prevent this illness from consuming me?"

Verity examined my mother, a thoughtful expression on her face. "There are a few remedies I'd suggest."

"Excellent," my mother said, cheering slightly. "What do you recommend I do first?" She leaned her elbows on the counter and put on her best listening face.

"Lemons are amazingly helpful," Verity said.

Aunt Thora's shoulders straightened. "Naturally."

"Do I put it in my tea with honey?" my mother asked. "That's not much of a potion. Humans do that every day."

"Well, you can," Verity said, "but my secret druid remedy involves taking a slice of lemon and using it to wipe all the affected areas. The more juice, the more effective."

"Even my eyes?" my mother asked. She touched the puffy areas on her face. "Won't that sting?"

"Only for a minute," Verity said, spooning oatmeal into Ryan's eager mouth. "It'll be worth it, though."

My mother smiled sweetly at Aunt Thora. "Do you mind if I use a lemon from the garden?"

"Choose carefully," she replied. "They've not all recovered."

"I thought you put a ward around the trees," I said.

"It didn't work," Aunt Thora said. "We're trying something else."

Now that her problem had been addressed, my mother

seemed ready to focus on those around her. "You're holding that spoon wrong, Verity, sweetheart."

My sister-in-law shot her a quizzical look. "The spoon?"

My mother zigzagged her finger. "The angle is wrong for his mouth."

"Are you sure he should be eating already?" Grandma asked. "Isn't he still explosive?"

"He can eat this," Verity said.

"He's a year old," Grandma said. "He should really be feeding himself."

"He has the rest of his life to feed himself," Aunt Thora said.

"Until he's old and toothless," Grandma said. "Then it's back to this." She gestured to Verity and Ryan.

"Circle of life," Tomas said.

"Eden, you really should sit down," my mother said. "It's better for your digestion."

"I'm fine over here." The table was crowded anyway.

Disapproval knitted my mother's brow. "You'll end up gaining weight in your feet and Nyx knows you don't need those to get any bigger than they are."

"That's not how biology works," I said. I spooned oatmeal into my mouth and said a silent thank you for my aunt's culinary skills.

"I'll tell you how biology works," my mother said. "You're not the only one with an education around here, young lady. Do you think they just hand out black magic certificates to anyone with the right hat?"

I squinted at her. "There's a right hat?"

"There's always a right hat," my mother said. "You'd know that if you ever bothered to pay attention to fashion."

A pounding on the door interrupted whatever zinger my mother was mentally preparing.

"That sounds urgent," Tomas said.

Everyone continued to sit there.

"Why don't you answer it, Beatrice?" Grandma asked.

"I can't answer the door in my condition," my mother said. "Why don't you?"

"I'm an old woman," Grandma said. "Anything can happen between here and the door."

The pounding continued.

"Someone is very persistent," Uncle Moyer said.

I rolled my eyes. "I'll get it."

Princess Buttercup accompanied me to the door. A low growl escaped her before I even managed to open it.

"Hush," I told her. I cracked the door far enough to speak to the visitor. "Can I help you?"

The man on the porch was red-faced and agitated. "Somebody on this street sideswiped my car and I intend to find out who it is," he said. His body crackled with anger.

"I'm not aware of any incidents," I said. "Where was your car parked?"

He pointed toward the mouth of the cul-de-sac. "I just moved in and left my car on the street so the moving van could park in the driveway."

"Oh. You're Michael Bannon," I said. "Welcome to the neighborhood." Sort of.

"There's a deep scratch on the side of my car. I want someone to pay for that."

"How do you know it wasn't already there?" I asked. "Do you check your car for marks every morning?"

Behind me, Princess Buttercup growled again, catching Michael's attention. "You plan to sic your attack dog on me now? Some neighborhood I moved into. I should've known better than to buy a house on a street that misspells its own name."

My mouth tightened. "The original signmaker was illiterate and no one had the heart to correct him." I'd heard the story from Alice because it happened before my time. The Wentworths were one of the original Puritan families in Chipping Cheddar and this house was once part of their farm, so Alice was full of local knowledge. "Anyway, Princess Buttercup isn't an attack dog," I said.

He peered around me. "I have eyes. That's a Great Dane."

And if he had the Sight, he'd see Princess Buttercup was actually a hellhound—which would probably escalate the situation.

"Who is this?" My mother pushed her way forward. "I am Beatrice Fury, the owner of this house. Is there a problem?"

The new neighbor seemed taken aback by my mother's appearance. "You should really see someone about your face."

If my mother could have smited him right there on the front porch and gotten away with it, I think she would have.

"There is nothing wrong with my face," my mother said tersely. "I'm sick."

"This is Michael Bannon," I said. "He moved into Dudley's house. Someone allegedly swiped the side of his car and he seeks recompense."

"Don't you use those big words with me, young lady," Michael said. "I know what you're up to."

My mother waved a dismissive hand. "Eden's always like that. Showing off her vocabulary. That's what happens when your looks aren't your best feature."

"Yes, it's tragic when a woman is forced to engage her brain," I said, my tone dripping with sarcasm.

My mother's laugh tinkled. "Mr. Bannon, I'm sorry about your car, but I'm afraid we don't know anything about it."

"And I suggest you don't go around accusing your new neighbors of property damage," Grandma chimed in from behind us. "It's a surefire way of alienating everyone."

Michael looked over our heads at her. "And you look like

an expert on alienating people, at least the male half of the population."

I heard a sharp intake of breath and realized it was mine. No one insulted Grandma and got away with it. I braced myself for payback, but Grandma remained surprisingly quiet. That wasn't necessarily a good thing either.

"I'm going to set up a security camera," Michael continued. "If I see anyone on this street near my property, I'm calling the police."

"Go ahead, honey," my mother said. "We've got nothing to hide."

To be fair, we had an awful lot to hide, but damage to Michael Bannon's car wasn't on the list.

"Go knock next door," Grandma urged. "I bet it was Mrs. Paulson. When she drives, it's like Miss Daisy decided to swipe the keys and go for a joyride."

Michael scowled one last time before stomping off in the direction of the neighbor's house.

"Grandma, you shouldn't have done that," I said. "He'll frighten her."

"Only if we're lucky," Grandma said.

"I can't believe how rude he was," my mother said, as we returned to the kitchen. "Can you imagine moving into a new neighborhood and treating others like that?"

"We ought to teach him a lesson," Grandma said.

"No," I said quickly. "No lessons."

"Why not?" Grandma asked. "When I was a young witch, if somebody got out of line, we made sure to help them with an attitude adjustment."

"I think Eden could use one of those," my mother said.

I cut her a quick glance. "Hey!" I objected.

"Your ego has gotten out of control," my mother said.

"My ego?" I repeated, gobsmacked.

"You defeat one measly demon and it's like you've invented Crest Whitestrips," my mother continued.

"One demon?" I asked. "I think this cold has infected your brain."

"Is there a problem?" Uncle Moyer asked. "I heard angry voices, but I know you can handle yourselves."

"No problem at all," I said. "And no one will be adjusting anyone's attitude or I'll be forced to file an FBM report. Am I clear?" I leveled a gaze at my mother and grandmother.

My mother patted my shoulder. "That's my girl. Always sucking the fun out of every occasion."

"Better than sucking the blood out of your ex-husband," Grandma said.

"Yes, I'll leave that to that Sally," my mother said. "Although bleeding him dry has a certain appeal."

"Mom," I said.

My mother heaved a sigh. "Censorship in my own home. Whatever next?"

I waved to Uncle Moyer and Tomas. "It was great to see you. Feel free to rake my father over the coals in about ten minutes."

My mother tapped her nail against her chin. "Now there's one I haven't tried."

I hurried up to the attic to change before I gave my mother any more ideas.

CHAPTER SEVEN

IT WAS STILL EARLY, so I decided to drop in at my dad and Sally's before I headed downtown to the office. It was a childhood habit that started after my parents divorced and my dad built the house next door. Anytime one parent spoke ill of the other one, I'd feel compelled to play the role of good daughter to the "victim." I'd bounce between houses, trying to assuage guilt that I shouldn't have felt in the first place.

"Sally, can I please come in?" I banged on the kitchen door at the back of the house.

Sally's wrinkle-free face appeared behind the beveled glass of the door. "Are you sick?"

"No. I'm heading to work soon and wanted to say hi to my dad."

Sally appeared unconvinced. "I heard about the epidemic that's sweeping this town. Someone died."

"What does it matter?" I asked. "You're already dead." Not that it mattered. Sally was a neat freak and a germaphobe. Her undead status was secondary.

"Did you touch Ryan today?" she asked.

"No," I said. "He was in a protective bubble most of the morning." I decided to keep my mother's condition to myself.

My father's face appeared beside Sally's. "When's the last time you checked the oil in your car?"

I frowned. "What does that have to do with being sick?"

"Nothing," he said. "I just thought of it and didn't want to forget to remind you."

I leaned my forehead against the glass. "I don't need to check the oil."

"Listen here, young lady. Just because you're immortal now doesn't mean you don't check your own oil. It's only a dipstick."

I stared back at him. "It sure is."

Sally knocked on the glass. "You're leaving smudges."

"Then let me in," I said. "I have a tongue and I'm not afraid to use it." I pretended to lick the glass.

My father jerked open the door. "Come in, but don't touch any of the food. Sally's practicing for FromageFest."

I strode into the kitchen and inhaled the divine scent of baked cheese. "You mean Cheese-chella."

My father banged his fist into his open palm. "It's FromageFest and don't you forget it."

"You seem a little touchy about a festival of cheese."

"It's those millennials and they're trendy names," my father said. "They're taking over."

"Well, they are the rising generation," I said. "I think that makes a takeover inevitable." I sniffed the air. "Gruyere?"

"You always had a nose for cheese," my father said with a grunt of approval.

"It's baked caramelized onion dip with gruyere," Sally said. "I'm entering it in the cheese dip competition."

My stomach rumbled. "That sounds as wonderful as it smells."

"It's in the oven now," Sally said.

You'd never know the vampire had been baking—the kitchen was already spotless.

"How long until it's finished?" I asked. "I'm happy to test it out before I go to work if you need feedback."

"No, thank you," Sally said. "That won't be necessary."

"It's for a contest, right? Don't you want to know what other people think?"

Something unspoken passed between them.

"What?" I asked.

My father sighed. "Sally doesn't want your germs in her dip."

"I already told you I'm not sick," I said, exasperated. Did I need to offer blood test results?

"It's not because you might be sick," my father said. "It's because you double dip."

I sucked in air. "I do not!"

"Yes, you do," Sally said. "I've seen you do it with the artichoke dip and that hummus I served at game night."

"Even your nephew knows better than to double dip," my father pointed out.

"My nephew doesn't even know how to use a toilet," I snapped. "I seriously doubt he's mastered the art of appetizers."

"Why are you here?" my father asked.

"Why am I ever here?"

He looked at me askance. "Hiding from your mother again?"

"She woke up…" I nearly said "sick," but caught myself. "In a bad mood and then we had a run-in with the new neighbor."

"What kind of run-in?" my father asked.

"Michael Bannon came by because someone side-swiped his car," I said. "He wasn't very nice about it."

"I wouldn't be nice about it either," my father said.

"That's the vengeance demon I know and love," Sally cooed.

"But he doesn't know who's responsible," I said. "He was pretty rude. He insulted Grandma."

My father snorted. "He's living the dream."

"He'll be living a nightmare if he doesn't calm down," I said. "I still can't believe she let it slide."

My father gaped at me. "What do you mean?"

"I mean she didn't react," I said.

Sally clutched her pearl necklace. "That can't be good."

"I think she was probably distracted. Uncle Moyer and Tomas are there, plus my mother's...bad mood. There was a lot going on."

"For his sake, I hope you're right," my father said.

I glanced at the clock on the microwave. "I should go if I want to stop for coffee first. Duty calls."

"As long as it's not diaper duty," my father said. "Ryan's not allowed over here until he's back to normal. It's a shame, too. We were making real progress."

I cocked my head. "Progress on what?"

My father couldn't resist a proud smile. "Last week, I saw him playing with his Lego figures and they were attacking each other."

I frowned. "Which ones?"

My father blew a dismissive raspberry. "Who knows? It's not like they have names."

"One wore all black with a matching helmet and the other one was all in white," Sally said.

"Sounds like Darth Vader and Luke Skywalker," I said. "They're supposed to fight each other."

"Yes, but the black helmet guy won," my father said. "It was a fierce battle, too, let me tell you. The kid has a strategic eye."

Sally stroked his arm. "He may have had a bit of help."

"Only a little," my father said. "I showed him how to take off the head, but the rest he did by himself."

I didn't want to know what "the rest" entailed. "He's a prodigy in the making," I said.

"I hope so, because it seems to have skipped a generation," my father said.

On that note... "Good luck with the cheese dip, Sally," I said. "I'll see you both later." I headed for the door.

"Just FYI, I'll be out of town for a day or so," my father said.

I stopped short. "Business or pleasure?"

"You know it's both for me," my father said. "When you love what you do, you never work a day in your life."

How anyone could love exacting revenge on someone else's enemy, I'd never understand.

"Safe travels," I said, because anything else would morph into an argument.

Half an hour later, I entered the office, clutching a large latte from Magic Beans, and stopped short when I noticed Neville at his desk.

"Are you preparing to scrub in, Doctor?" I asked.

Neville typed away on his computer, wearing a surgical mask and gloves. He removed the mask to speak. "I have a delicate system. I can't afford to be exposed to whatever's going around."

"I'll do my best to cough into my elbow."

"I'm not sure that will be enough for this potent infection."

"We don't know what killed him yet," I said. "It could be an overdose of medicine or drugs. Could be a preexisting condition." I sat in my chair and switched on the computer.

"Could be the next bubonic plague," Neville said.

"There's looking on the bright side," I said. "Did you hear about the singer on the police scanner?" The "police scanner" is actually a magical listening device he'd installed in the police chief's office to stay on top of crimes and investigations.

"Only this morning," Neville said. "I played back the recording when I got here. According to the report, you called it in."

"Sure did," I said. "That's what happens when I try to have a normal night, Neville. Someone dies."

"Someone else died," he said.

I spun around in my chair to face him. "What?"

"A car accident early this morning on the outskirts of town."

"How is this connected to the singer's death? Did someone sneeze and accidentally drive into a tree?"

"Not to my knowledge," he said.

"Well, does it have a supernatural connection?"

"Not unless the deer that ran out in front of the car was actually a werewolf."

I stiffened. "Is there any way to know for sure?"

"I believe the deer carcass on the side of the road tells us for sure."

I turned back to my computer. "Then why are you telling me about it? I don't get involved in routine deaths." Gods, that sounded horrible, even to my own ears.

"You got involved last night," Neville said.

"Only because I happened to be there."

"And because a certain police chief would be coming to the scene to file a report?"

I glared at him over my shoulder. "It wasn't a date, Neville. It was a death." I didn't dare mention our detour afterward and risk the gentle clucking of the wizard's disapproving tongue.

I decided to be productive in order to force thoughts of Chief Fox out of my head.

"Are today's reports in from Otherworld?"

"No escaped or missing demons today," Neville replied.

"Well, that's a plus." I sneezed and grabbed a tissue from the box on my desk in the nick of time. "Fast reflexes are good for something."

Neville quickly replaced his mask.

"It was one sneeze, Neville. Probably seasonal allergies."

"I'd rather take precautions," came his muffled reply.

My phone began to play the Exorcist theme song.

"That sounds scary," Neville said.

"Because it is." I stared at the screen for another beat before deciding to answer. "What is it, Mom? You know I'm at work."

"Can you please bring home some medicine from the drugstore?"

"You want human medicine?" I asked. "Why?"

"Because our potions aren't working and the only thing Verity's lemon remedy did was burn the hell out of me," she complained.

I had a feeling that was exactly the outcome Verity expected.

"I still feel awful. Bring me every bottle in the cold and flu aisle."

"It's only been a few hours," I said. "These things can take time."

"I don't have time," my mother said. "I'm supposed to go out with Jeremiah tonight."

I didn't bother to ask who Jeremiah was. It was doubtful I'd ever hear the name again anyway.

"I don't think you should go out with anyone until you're better," I said.

"You just don't want me to enjoy myself," my mother snapped. "After everything I've done for you."

"Do you really want Jeremiah to see you like this?" I asked. "Remember Michael Bannon's reaction when he saw you." It was a low blow, but I knew it would pack the necessary punch.

My mother hesitated. "I'm sure I could do a spell…"

"Cancel the date," I said. "And I'll bring you medicine when I come home later."

"This is extortion," my mother huffed.

I blew a breath. "It's nothing like extortion."

"Eden Joy Fury…"

I hung up before she could finish her sentence.

"Exactly how sick is your mother?" Neville asked.

"She's a drama queen so it's hard to judge," I said.

"Isn't your nephew sick as well?"

I cut him a quick glance. "Relax, Neville. It's nothing to get worked up about. Verity is running blood tests. If it's anything serious, I'll let you know."

"Perhaps we should review our demon summaries from last week," Neville suggested. "Keep our minds occupied while we wait."

"I don't need to keep my mind occupied," I said.

"But you do need to review," Neville said. "We promised Agent Redmond that we'd continue practical exercises. The demon summaries are part of that."

"And I intend to keep that promise," I said. "As soon as I finish rearranging my sock drawer."

"Agent Fury, you were highly regarded by the FBI. Why do you resist applying the same work ethic to the FBM?"

I refused to look at him. "You know why."

"The fact is that you're here now and you've already managed to have an impact," the wizard said. "Why not fully embrace it?"

I swiveled around in my chair to face him. "I guess I keep hoping that the FBI will change their mind and ask me to come back. That I won't have to stay."

Neville frowned. "You realize that's completely unrealistic at this point, don't you?"

"Hope isn't necessarily realistic."

"Would you really go back to San Francisco if you were given the opportunity?" he asked. "What about Chief Fox?"

"What about him?" I shot back. "I'm not able to be in a relationship with him."

"No, but you're able to watch out for him and save him from supernatural threats he's oblivious to," Neville said. "How would you do that from across the country?"

"Paul Pidcock didn't have to do that for Chief O'Neill," I said.

Neville leaned back against his chair. "Have you forgotten how Mick O'Neill died?"

"Of course not." The former chief of police died at the hands of the same demon that killed Paul Pidcock.

"The portal may be dormant, but the fact remains that Chipping Cheddar is a magnet for supernaturals," Neville said. "We have our very own vortex. Without someone in this post with your capabilities, Agent Fury, this town is likely to suffer preventable fatalities."

I picked up my pen and tapped the end rhythmically on the desk. "We've already suffered fatalities since I've been home."

"And think of how many more there might've been without you."

It wasn't a number I cared to contemplate.

My phone buzzed and I pulled it from my pocket to see Verity's name. "Hi. Everything okay?"

"Where are you?"

"At my office," I said.

"Oh, good." Her relief was palpable. "That's the best place for you right now."

"That sounds ominous. What's up?"

"Bad news," Verity said. "I got the test results and you're not going to like it."

"Is it Lyme disease?" Those little bloodsucking ticks have nothing on vampires, as far as I'm concerned.

"No."

"Malaria?" Mosquitoes are minions straight from hell.

"It's not an earthly disease. The cause is supernatural."

Double-decker crap sandwich. "You're sure?"

"Yes. Have you heard from the chief yet about the singer's autopsy report?"

"No, it's too soon," I said. The body had been transported to Baltimore where the Office of the Chief Medical Examiner is located.

"I guarantee you that report won't show anything unusual," Verity said.

"So you think it's the same infection?" I asked.

"Yes. I suspect that's why it killed the human," Verity replied. "Supernaturals have more resistance to their own infections."

"This thing seems to be spreading quickly, though," I said. "That means the human population is at risk."

"Which means you need to figure out the source and how to stop it," Verity said.

"Is there anything else you can tell me?" I asked.

"Only that it's likely to be an Otherworld strain," Verity said. "I've never seen it here before and it was potent enough to kill a healthy, young male."

My gears were clicking away. "So someone could've brought it back from Otherworld as a carrier and then spread it here?" If that was the case, my own father could be the culprit. He was constantly back and forth between realms due to his job, although the trip he mentioned today was the first one in a couple of weeks, so his involvement was unlikely.

"It's possible there's a Patient Zero and they don't even realize it," Verity said.

"The band," I said suddenly. "Three of them are supernaturals and the drummer was also sick." And still alive.

"One of my nurses told me there's a tribute to Ray Langdon downtown later," Verity said. "I'm sure the rest of the band will be here."

"Not ideal if the werewolf is responsible for spreading this," I said. "Thanks for letting me know." I hung up the phone and turned to see Neville with his surgical mask back on.

"You think the drummer might have brought back a souvenir from Otherworld?" his muffled voice asked.

"I don't know," I said, "but that's what I intend to find out."

CHAPTER EIGHT

I ARRIVED at Pimento Plaza where a makeshift stage had been erected in front of the statue of Arthur Davenport. The plaza is one of the most attractive parts of town, surrounded by pretty historical buildings with the Chesapeake Bay as a backdrop. Under different circumstances, I'd be happy to be here.

"Eden, I didn't expect to see you here," Clara said. "I would've picked you up."

"I'm not here for fun," I said.

Clara cocked her head. "No one is. It's a tribute." She reached for my arm and seemed to feel the stress and uncertainty swirling inside me. "Is there something you want to tell me?"

My gaze flicked to Sassy. "Not right now. Maybe later."

"I am not wearing one of those stupid masks," Sassy said. "It completely covers one of my best features."

"Your nose?" Clara asked.

"And my mouth," Sassy added. "Basically anything that covers a portion of my face is a loss for humanity."

"I'll bear that in mind while we listen to the band's tribute." As they mourn an actual loss to humanity.

As I surveyed the plaza, it seemed that Neville wasn't alone in his paranoia. People were wearing surgical masks and standing an arm's length apart. Instead of waving phones and lighters in the air, they held citronella candles. Apparently, I wasn't the only one to blame mosquitoes.

"Need a spritz?" a young woman asked through her surgical mask. She held one of those small bottles with a fan that sprayed water that I'd seen at amusement parks and the beach.

"You want to spray me with water?" Sassy asked. "I mean, as sexy as I look when I'm wet, it's not that hot outside."

The young woman shook the bottle. "It's not water. It's antibacterial gel. Just make sure to close your eyes."

"We'll pass, thanks," I said.

I scanned the faces in the crowd and recognized the drummer, whose bright red nose suggested she still had the cold symptoms, but at least she was still alive. She could thank her supernatural blood for that.

"The vibe here is super low-key," Sassy said. "Where's the energy?"

"Do I need to explain what a tribute is?" I asked.

"It's when they play songs someone else wrote," Sassy said.

Clara and I exchanged glances.

"She's not wrong," Clara said.

"Okay, in some circumstances, that's true," I said. "However, Ghost of Billy Crystal is playing tonight in honor of Ray, their lead singer." I paused, waiting for the news to register. Sassy's expression remained blank.

"He died in the middle of a performance," Clara added.

Understanding rippled across Sassy's perfect features. "Oh, *that* guy."

Clara shook her head. "You really need to start paying attention."

"When did you tell me?" Sassy asked.

"When we were standing out front of the office and I mentioned going to the tribute tonight," Clara said.

Sassy snapped her fingers. "That's when I spotted Ian across the street washing windows."

Clara looked at her expectantly. "And?"

Sassy shrugged. "And he's hot. Sorry, I got distracted. His shirt was off."

If ever two people deserved each other, it was Sassy and Tanner. The more time I spent with her, the more convinced I became. As much as his betrayal hurt, I dodged a diseased bullet with that guy.

"I have extra masks if you want," a guy offered. He held out a couple of masks by their ties.

Clara reached for one.

"Five bucks," he said, snapping it back.

Clara yanked her hand away. "Criminal!"

He smiled. "Capitalist."

I started to think the masks weren't such a bad idea for Sassy and Clara. If they were more susceptible to whatever disease this was, I wanted to protect them.

"Hey, capitalist." I flashed my FBM badge, which identified me as FBI to human eyes. "I need two masks."

His gaze darted to the shiny badge. "Sure thing. Sorry about that." He tossed the masks at us and disappeared into the crowd.

The tribute for Ray kicked off with the remaining band members playing a few songs, including *It's A Shame About Ray* by the Lemonheads, and I couldn't decide whether that was in poor taste or genius.

"Eden, what are you doing here?" My cousin Meg wove her way through the empty space between bodies to reach us.

"Same as you, I expect," I said. "Paying my respects."

"They were such a good band," Meg said. "I saw them play at a bonfire a few months ago."

I noticed she held an old-fashioned sparkler, still unlit. "That's your light?"

Meg glanced at the stick in her hand. "I'm saving it for the end."

Despite her teen status, Meg eschewed technology, much to her mother's dismay. Julie wanted to be able to keep constant tabs on her daughter, a goal that technology definitely supported.

"If you have any human friends here with you," I said in a low voice, "I'd encourage them to go home and avoid crowds for the time being."

Meg's eyes widened slightly. "You mean these masks aren't overkill?"

"I don't want people to overreact," I said, "but until I know more, that's what I recommend."

Meg nodded solemnly and slipped back between the throng of bodies.

"I'm bored," Sassy announced.

"The music's about to finish. Why don't you take her home?" I said to Clara.

She got the message. "We've paid our respects. I don't mind leaving."

I gave her a grateful smile before turning toward the band. They were about to finish their final song and I wanted to swoop in and speak to the drummer before they were inundated with mourners.

"Yvette," I called from beside the makeshift stage. When she turned in my direction, I flashed my badge.

She hit the drums with one last flourish and hopped off the stage before anyone could intercept her.

"I'm Agent Fury," I said. "I'd like to ask you a few questions."

"Ray died of natural causes," Yvette said. "Why would the FBM get involved?"

"It's about your cold," I said.

Yvette pulled out a tissue and blew her nose. "I can't get rid of it. I've taken every tonic and potion in the pack dispensary. Nothing's helping."

"Have you taken any trips lately? Maybe a visit to Otherworld?"

Yvette's eyes popped. "Otherworld? I've never set foot there. It's not like going to another state, you know. It's not even like going to another country. There are all sorts of restrictions and paperwork."

I held up a hand. "I'm familiar with the bureaucracy, thanks." A few people tried to come over to talk to her and I waited to continue.

"I'll see you in a minute," she said and shooed them away.

"How about anyone you spend time with?" I asked.

Yvette shook her head. "I don't know anyone with ties to Otherworld. What's this really about?"

"This sickness," I said. "It's not from this world. It's a supernatural strand. That's why Ray died."

Yvette gasped. "How? How would we be infected by something from another realm?"

"That's what I'm trying to piece together. In the meantime, I'd like you to pay a visit to my sister-in-law tomorrow. Dr. Verity Fury. She'll take a blood sample and confirm."

Yvette's head bobbed up and down and I could tell she was still digesting the information. "Am I danger to society?"

"I would recommend that you avoid contact as much as possible."

"Is there something I can take?"

"Until we know exactly what we're dealing with, I don't know that she can recommend anything that will help."

Yvette looked around at all the people gathered in the plaza. "I'm going to sneak home now. I don't want to put anyone at risk."

"Humans are in the most danger," I said. "Their immune systems aren't equipped to handle it."

"Thank you for letting me know," Yvette said.

"If you hear of anyone else, send them to Dr. Verity, not the human doctor." Unfortunately, no human would be able to help them.

"I will." Yvette blew her nose one more time before fleeing into an alley, away from the crowd.

I arrived home to find a familiar figure on the porch. "Mr. Bannon?"

He turned to look at me. Even in the dim light, I could see that his face was haggard and his eyes lined with red.

The front door opened, revealing Grandma in her fuzzy robe and slippers. I was beginning to wonder if something— or someone—had happened to her wardrobe.

"Someone keeps ringing my doorbell," he said.

"So answer it like I did," Grandma said. "It's easy."

Michael dragged a hand through his thinning hair. "You don't understand. I've been answering it, but no one's there. I think my house might be haunted."

It wasn't beyond belief, considering my mother's house was technically haunted. Alice wasn't any kind of threat, though. Because I was the only one who could see and hear Alice, it seemed only natural that we became friends.

Grandma cackled. "I don't think so. Dudley left that house in a box, but that's only because his car is the size of a postage stamp."

"It might be kids," I offered. "Sometimes they like to play pranks." Although we didn't have many kids of that age in the cul-de-sac.

"I thought that, too," Michael said, "but my security camera isn't picking up anyone. The bell rings, but no one's there."

"A mechanical malfunction then," I said.

Michael nodded. "Yeah, you're probably right. I'll call an electrician."

"Sound like a good plan," Grandma said. "Good luck to you." She shut the door before he could say anything else and left me standing on the porch with him.

"I regret moving to this neighborhood," Michael said. "The people are strange."

"People are strange everywhere," I said.

He scrutinized me. "Only a strange person would say that."

"You really have a way of insulting people," I said. I patted his arm. "You'll fit in better than you think." I left him on the porch and went inside, careful to avoid the common areas. I zipped straight to the attic before anyone could intervene.

"Alice, are you watching *Wonder Woman* again?" I demanded. Her transparent body hovered in front of the television in the attic.

"It's female empowerment at its finest." Alice gestured to the screen where Wonder Woman was lifting a car over her head. "Can you do that?"

"I don't know," I said. "I've never tried."

"You should carry a sword like hers," Alice said. "It would really add to your overall look."

I smoothed my sides. "I don't need an overall look. Besides, people might get a little nervous if I start walking around town with a sword."

"You should at least consider magic bracelets," Alice said. She touched her wrist. "They're so handy in a crisis."

"I'll take it under advisement. Listen, are you aware of any other ghosts in the neighborhood?" I asked.

"On Munster Close?" Alice asked.

"One of the new neighbors is having an issue," I said. I explained the doorbell situation.

"I don't think there are any ghosts in Chipping Cheddar who would bother with such shenanigans."

"Due to their busy schedules?" I asked wryly.

"Due to their integrity and maturity," Alice said.

"Oh," I said. "We don't really have that here."

Alice kept her eyes on the screen. "He doesn't seem like a very nice man. I'll say that much."

"No, not much of a charmer."

"How was the tribute?" Alice asked.

"Helpful. Turns out the sickness is supernatural, probably from Otherworld. Unfortunately, Yvette's never been to Otherworld, so she's not Patient Zero."

"Wow. You've been busy today," Alice said.

"And here I thought it was nothing to be concerned about."

Alice's mouth formed a tiny 'o.'

"What is it?" I asked.

"Olivia's sick," the ghost said. "She came home from school with a fever and congestion."

"The good news is that supernaturals seem to be more resistant," I said. "It's the humans we need to worry about."

"In that case, you should worry about John because he's sick, too."

I froze. "John Maclaren?"

"Yes. He sent a text to your mother earlier, letting her know he wouldn't be here tomorrow to work on the barn."

I shook off my nerves. "It could still be a regular cold or

allergies." Even so, I'd make sure Verity took a blood sample.

Alice folded her arms. "I suppose you ought to suit up, Agent Fury. Agent assemble!"

"First, there's no suit. Second, there's only one agent, so I can't assemble. You need a group in order to assemble." I glanced helplessly at the screen. "Go easy on the superhero movies, okay? Maybe try *The Sound of Music* or something."

As much as I preferred to hide in the attic away from my family, I needed to talk to Verity and check on Olivia and Ryan. I didn't worry about my mother. She'd survive the apocalypse. Hell, she'd probably cause the apocalypse.

I found Verity and Anton in the family room, snuggled on the couch. "Where's everyone else?"

"They've gone to bed early," Verity said. "Olivia wore everyone out with her demands before she fell asleep."

"How is she?" I asked.

"She seems to be fully functional, other than her symptoms," Verity said. "I'm trying not to be overly concerned. Like I told you, I think supernaturals can ride it out."

"John's sick," I said.

Anton straightened. "The carpenter?"

"Yeah."

Anton swore softly.

The sound of my phone jolted me. "Who changed my ringtone to *You Sexy Thing*?" I plucked the phone from my pocket.

"I can think of at least two suspects," Verity said.

"Hello?"

"Good evening, Agent Fury. I hope it's not too late to call."

My heart hammered in my chest. "No, it's fine."

"Not on a date then?"

"I'm in the family room with Anton and Verity, so I'll let you work that one out."

"I said I'd let you know when I got the autopsy report."

"Let me guess. Natural causes," I said.

"How'd you know?"

"Just a hunch."

"His medical records were clean, too. His last physical was only three months ago." The chief sighed. "Sometimes it's plain bad luck."

And sometimes there's an intervening cause that even the most capable humans can't see. "Thanks for letting me know, Chief."

"No problem. We're a team, remember?"

"We're really not, but I appreciate being kept in the loop." I clicked off the phone.

"It's difficult to keep things from him," Verity said.

"For many reasons," I replied.

"He could be helpful," Verity said.

"It's too dangerous," I said. "Mick O'Neill was chief for how many years? He never had a clue and he managed just fine."

"Until he died of supernatural causes," Verity said.

My head dropped. "Yeah. I made the same point to Neville. Even if Chief O'Neill had known the truth, though, it doesn't mean that knowledge would have saved him. He never even saw the demon that killed him."

"He would've had a stroke long before that demon killed him," Anton said. "His job would've been exponentially harder with that information. I liked Mick a lot, but I don't think he could've handled the truth."

Verity looked up at him. "And what about Chief Fox?"

"It's not for me to say," Anton said. "I'd leave that one to Eden to decide."

"The only decision Eden is going to make right now is to go to bed," I said. I felt exhausted by the day's events and hoped a good night's sleep would put me in the right mindset to prevent a few flurries from becoming a storm.

CHAPTER NINE

"Great balls of a minotaur," I croaked, opening my eyes—
or trying to. They were puffy and crusty. Terrific.

"Oh, Eden, you look…" Alice hovered over my bed. Her
concerned expression told me what I needed to know.

"How bad is it?" I asked. I drew myself to a seated position and immediately sneezed. "Ow, my back."

"You're far too young to be pulling muscles when you
sneeze," Alice scolded me.

"I'll be sure to pass the message along to my central
control system." I tapped my head.

"Do you think it's the deadly disease?" Alice asked.

I swung my legs over the side of the mattress. "It's not a
deadly disease. Not for me."

"Someone died," Alice said.

"Someone also died yesterday from falling down the
steps," I said. "I'm not about to declare steps a deadly menace
to society."

"You're underplaying this so as not to worry," Alice said.

I fixed her with a resentful stare. "Now you're a shrink?"

"Maybe you should try your mother's remedy with the

lemon," Alice said. She paused. "On second thought, don't. It didn't help and seemed quite painful."

I broke into a huge smile. "You saw her?"

"The bathroom door was open and I happened by." Alice shook her ghostly head. "The scream was enough to pierce my heart."

I laughed. "I'm so sorry I missed that." I sneezed again and reached for the tissue box positioned on one of the storage containers. "I guess I'll carry this with me today. I promised Neville I'd do a training session."

"Try not to worry," Alice said. "We suffered through an outbreak or two in my time. There were serious casualties, but many lived."

I changed out of my pajamas and threw on yoga pants and a T-shirt. "You really need to work on your pep talk." I sneezed again and howled in pain as I pulled another muscle.

"At least you're not urinating in your pants," Alice said. "That's what happens when your grandmother sneezes."

My head jerked toward her. "Please say that again."

"Sneezing seems to trigger her bladder."

I bolted from the mattress.

"Where are you going?" Alice asked.

A slow smile emerged. "To spend a little quality time with Grandma before I have to leave for work."

I came downstairs to find the remaining family members gathered in the kitchen, mid-conversation.

"Well, I don't want to ride over to nurse him back to health," my mother said.

Grandma arched an eyebrow. "Since when?"

My mother futzed with loose strands of hair around her face. "What if he doesn't like what he sees?"

"Your face looks back to normal," I said. "Did you use a spell?"

My mother batted her eyelashes. "A witch never reveals her secrets."

"Looks like you're in need of a spell," Grandma said. She pointed to my face. "I haven't seen that much crust since Thora volunteered to bake for the pie eating competition."

"It's not me I'm concerned about," I said.

"Mark this day down in history, ladies and gentlemen," my mother said. "Eden's not concerned with herself."

"She means because the infection seems to be supernatural in origin," Aunt Thora interjected. "Verity told us yesterday."

"I just knew it was a mystical event," my mother said. "My body's felt heavy with magic ever since I started feeling unwell."

"Those are your boobs," Grandma said. "They're more like bags of cement than flotation devices."

"Better than empty tube socks," my mother shot back.

"Where are Olivia and Ryan?" I asked.

"In bed," my mother said. "Aunt Thora is going to stay with them, although I'm thinking it's best if I don't leave the house like this."

Finally, my mother made sense.

"Since when do you suffer from a crisis of confidence?" Grandma asked.

My mother pursed her lips. "I know I'm flawed. It's time to face reality."

I stared at her, beginning to question my own reality. "This infection is infecting your brain."

"That doesn't sound like you, Beatrice," Aunt Thora said.

"No kidding," Grandma interjected. "You spend the night crumbling men to dust and then sprinkle them on your cereal the next morning for added flavor."

I cringed at the mental image. "Did something happen to trigger this revelation?"

"Sure something happened," Grandma said. "She finally cleaned the mirror in her bathroom."

My mother stared daggers at Grandma. "I have a pimple," she blurted.

"Where?" I scanned her face for any sign of a red bump.

My mother shied away. "On my buttocks."

"How would you even know such a thing?" I closed my eyes. "Wait. Please don't answer that."

"The carpenter isn't going to see a zit on your ass," Grandma said. "You're delivering soup, not sex."

Aunt Thora ladled soup from a pot into a container. "My homemade chicken noodle soup is as close to sex as you can get."

"Wait," I said. "You're talking about bringing soup to John? You can't do that."

"No need to be jealous," my mother said.

"I'm not jealous, but you can't risk making him any sicker," I said.

"He's already been exposed," my mother said. "There's no harm now."

"We have no idea how this disease works," I said. "Do you really want to risk John's life just so you can play Florence Nightingale?"

My mother admired her reflection in the microwave. "I do look ravishing in a nurse's uniform. Might be worth it to him."

Inwardly, I groaned.

"You don't have time for home deliveries, Eden," Grandma said. "You need to get to the bottom of this mess. That's your job."

"Right now my job is to meet Neville in the park for a training exercise," I said.

"How can you focus on exercise when there's an epidemic in the works?" my mother asked.

"We're not jogging," I said. "It's training. It helps me prepare for the next crisis."

Grandma secured the lid on the soup container. "I don't see how skipping around in a field prepares you for an outbreak, but what do I know? I'm just an old woman."

"I'll drop off the soup," I said. "I'll leave it on the front step so I don't put him at further risk."

Grandma held the container against her chest. "I'll take the soup. There's nothing wrong me."

"I beg to differ" my mother murmured.

"Fine," I said. "Just don't linger in case your symptoms aren't showing yet." I grabbed my car keys from the counter. "Try to steer clear of humanity for now."

"Only for now?" my mother asked.

I flashed an impertinent smile. "One battle at a time."

Today's battle was entirely make-believe.

"Are you seriously going to wear that during our entire training session?"

Neville cowered behind an oak tree in Davenport Park, wearing the surgical mask and gloves that had basically become his new uniform.

"What does it matter?" he shouted from behind the mask. "I don't need my face and hands exposed in order to be effective."

I cupped my hand to my ear. "What was that? I couldn't hear your life-or-death instructions because of that piece of fabric in front of your mouth."

His brow knitted in what I assumed was a scowl—hard to be certain when I couldn't see his whole face. He pulled down the mask. "You know the drill, Agent Fury." He quickly replaced the mask over his mouth.

"I'm the one who's already sick," I said, coughing for good

measure. "If anyone should be skittish right now, it's me."

"I won't object if you want to cancel training today," Neville said. "Your health is of the upmost importance."

"Sedentary isn't my thing." I spread my arms wide. "We're in the great outdoors, Neville. Fresh air and sunshine will blow the cobwebs away."

"I'll stay here with the mighty oak, thank you." He dangled a pouch where I could see it. "Are you ready for your opponent?"

"How many more subjects do I need to defeat to reach level five?" I asked.

"Three," Neville said. "Though I'm not sure you should expend the effort today. Maybe just take on the first one and leave the next two until you've fully recovered."

"You don't have to baby me." I anchored my feet and clapped my hands together. "Ready when you are."

Neville tossed the magic dust into the air, which triggered a succession of sneezes from me. Through my dewy eyes, I saw a demon take shape. I fished a tissue from my pocket and blew my nose.

"He's pretty," I said. For once, I wasn't being sarcastic. The demon reminded me of a tropical fish with brightly colored skin and a Mohawk-like hairdo.

"It's all well and good to admire him, Agent Fury, but you should really focus on identification and defeat."

"Right." I stuffed the tissue back into my pocket and concentrated on the demon. "This one's easy to remember."

Neville sighed. "The pretty ones always are."

I pointed at my new friend. "You're a discus demon."

He growled in response and advanced toward me. It was then that I remembered what discus demons are known for.

"You shoot acid!" I ducked just in time as a stream of hissing liquid passed over my head, narrowly missing my scalp. "Your drool is worse than Princess Buttercup's!"

"You might want to consider skipping the banter if you want to reach level five today," Neville called.

"I think you might be right about not pushing it." I tried to remember what I'd read about discus demons. A-ha! "They can dish it out, but they can't take it."

Neville appeared confused. "He's not bantering. You are."

As the discus demon stalked toward me, I started to cough. I held out a hand to still his movements. "He's not stopping!"

"I don't have a remote control for him, Agent Fury," Neville called. "You'll have to fight."

The demon continued toward me as my coughing intensified. I suddenly regretted my need for overachievement. What did I have to prove anyway?

Another stream of acid shot toward me and I dropped to the ground and somersaulted to avoid the scorching liquid.

"There's something you should know about me," I said, popping up right in front of him. "I have a lot of experience with acid tongues." Before he could respond, I placed a hand on his arm and activated my siphoning power. Of course, my stupid cold decided to rear its ugly head again and I sneezed acid right in his face. His colorful skin burned and he staggered backward. I gave him one more hit of acid—not the good kind—and he dissipated.

I dropped to the ground and landed squarely on my bottom. "Ouch! Why do we still have tailbones? What's the point?"

Neville left the safety of the tree to check on me. He held out a gloved hand and pulled me to my feet. "Are you prepared to call it a day?"

"Fine," I relented. "This cold is kicking my butt harder than any demon anyway." My butt vibrated and I pulled out my phone. "Hi, Verity."

"You need to head over to the nursing home," the druid said. "There's a reported case. Henrietta Egerrton."

My stomach clenched. The elderly would be defenseless against a supernatural strain. "I'm on my way." I put away the phone and looked at the paranoid wizard. "Hey, Neville. How about I borrow your mask?"

I drove across town to the nursing home, trying to remain calm. My father used to threaten my grandmother with a room here when my parents were still married. In turn, my grandmother threatened him with castration, so they worked out a peaceful coexistence for the most part. When my parents divorced and my father moved out, the stress level definitely decreased. My family never made any effort to hide their discontent. Hexes and vengeance spells were a regular feature of my childhood—and my adulthood.

I parked the car and entered the lobby of the nursing home. I was surprised to see a familiar—and unwelcome—face among the other visitors.

"Eden Fury, what are you doing here?" Tanner's mother, Gale Hughes, was affixing a name badge to her top.

"Same as you, I expect."

Her eyebrow arched. "You're visiting my mother?"

"Patrice is here?" I remembered Tanner's grandmother as a sweetheart—basically the polar opposite of her daughter.

"We moved her in here last year," Gale said. "Her dementia became an issue. She almost burned down the house with a tea kettle."

"I'm sorry to hear that," I said.

Gale observed me from head to toe. "You can't be visiting one of your own relatives. They'd never let a Fury take up residence here. Too much of a liability." Although Gale didn't know our true natures, you'd never know it by the way she talked about us. It was as though she had a sixth sense.

"I'm checking on a resident," I said, in an effort to keep my reason vague. No need to start a stampede out of the nursing home. "Nice to see you again."

Gale gave me a sour look before disappearing down the corridor.

I stepped up to the reception desk. "I'm here to see Henrietta Egerrton."

The young woman behind the desk beamed up at me. "Are you a relative?"

"No." I whipped out my badge and showed it to her. "Official business."

The young woman inclined her head, studying the badge. "Cool. I've never seen one of these up close. Should I notify the director?"

"That won't be necessary. I only need to have a conversation with her. I understand she's unwell."

The young woman hesitated. "Yeah, there's something going around." She opened the drawer and produced a visitor badge. "Wear this. She's in room 302. Down the hall and to the left."

I pinned the badge to my shirt. "Thank you."

I wandered down the corridor, narrowly avoiding getting my toes crushed by a passing wheelchair. For a sick woman, Henrietta certainly seemed spry. She sat up in bed, playing cards with two others—an elderly man with a paunch as round as his bald head and a woman with hair dyed so black, it looked like she'd dumped an inkwell on top of it.

"Whose turn is it?" the old man asked.

"No idea," the black-haired woman said. "Henrietta?"

"You think I remember?" Henrietta asked. "The only reason I remember we're playing is because I'm holding cards."

I knocked gently on the open door. "Excuse me. Are you Henrietta?"

The older woman in bed glanced at me. "Yes. Are you the doctor?"

"No, ma'am. My name is Agent Eden Fury. I'd like to talk to you about your symptoms."

She shrank back, holding her cards against her chest. "Is this a government conspiracy? I've heard all about those and I don't want any part of it."

"I'd just like to ask you about your cold," I said. "I won't even examine you. Promise."

"You can examine me," the elderly man said, wiggling his eyebrows. "I'll make it easy for you and undress myself."

"Kelvin, with your arthritis, you couldn't undress yourself if you were in a threesome with Marilyn Monroe and Hedy Lamarr."

He shrugged. "I wouldn't need to. I'd have two women there to do it for me."

"Such an ape." Henrietta chucked a card at Kelvin's head.

"Would you mind if I spoke with Ms. Egerrton privately?" I asked.

Her companions vacated the room and I maintained a careful distance. "I don't want to alarm you, but I'm going to put this mask on because I don't want to spread germs in here."

"I've got enough germs as it is," Henrietta said. "Why does the FBI care about my cold?"

"Just a precaution. Can you tell me when your symptoms started?"

Henrietta appeared thoughtful. "It was yesterday. I remember because I was relieved I didn't have any visitors. My grandson had come the day before, you see."

"Is he local?"

"Yes, he works at the bank downtown."

"Which one? Stilton Bank?"

"That's the one." She seemed pleased to remember. "He's working his way up to manager." She curled her fingers in her lap. "He loves working in the heart of town. He told me there's a new coffee place next door."

"Magic Beans. Does he like it?"

"Loves it. It saves him the walk to The Daily Grind. He only gets half an hour for his break. He'd rather not spend it walking."

"Can't blame him." I ventured closer to the bed but kept my mask intact. "Have you been seen by a doctor?"

"Oh yes. Dr. Barton. He's our regular one. Says it's only a nasty cold and that I should recover within the week."

"Was your grandson sick?" I asked.

"Not when he visited, but his mother told me this morning that he's fighting a cold, too."

"You haven't had any other visitors?"

"Only people who already live here," Henrietta said.

I hated to ask this of her because she probably felt isolated already, but I didn't have a choice. "Ms. Egerrton, I need to ask you an important favor."

"What is it, dear?"

"Stick to your room until your symptoms clear and try to avoid contact with anyone."

Henrietta frowned. "This is serious, isn't it?"

I decided to come as clean as I could. "It might be, and if it is, I don't want you to endanger yourself or anyone else."

She gave a slight nod. "I guess it's a good thing they left me the cards. That's a lot of solitaire practice."

"I'm sorry. If your symptoms get worse, please call Dr. Verity Fury. Don't wait."

"Oh, Dr. Barton has mentioned her. She's very good, isn't she?"

"She is. Take care, Ms. Egerrton."

"Be a dear and close the door behind you."

I did as instructed and removed my mask as I entered the corridor. On my way out, I recognized Patrice's voice coming from the room on my right. I poked my head inside. "Mrs. Sibbes?"

"Eden? Is that really you?" Tanner's grandmother was upright in her bed. Her thinning white hair was fastened with a barrette on either side, giving her a childlike appearance. Gale sat in a chair in the corner, scowling as I entered.

"It is." I hovered in the doorway. "You look wonderful. I like your hair."

Patrice's fingers brushed across one of the barrettes. "Sassy brought them for me. You remember Sassafras Persimmons, don't you? Such a sweet girl."

Gale smirked. "They know each other, Mamma."

Patrice's gaze seemed distant. "I hope she and Tanner get married soon. I'd like to live long enough to see my grandson get married."

"Can I get you anything?" I asked.

"No, dear, but thank you kindly." Patrice focused her big blue eyes on me. "I was sorry things didn't work out between you and Tanner. I've always been fond of you."

The immature part of me wanted to stick my tongue out at Tanner's disapproving mother.

"Mamma, you know they would never have worked out," Gale said. "Tanner is a special boy. He needs a special woman's touch."

"He's had a lot of special touches from women," Patrice said. "More than his fair share, I reckon." She giggled. "Suppose I shouldn't say that about my own grandson."

"Can he help it if women throw themselves at him?" Gale asked. "He's a handsome, successful young man. God broke the mold when He made my Tanner."

"Have you met the new chief of police?" Patrice asked. "Gale says he's quite attractive *and* an eligible bachelor."

"We've met," I said vaguely. No way was I going to get into details in front of Gale.

"I have to admit, it's a nice change to have a younger man looking out for our community," Gale said. "Mick O'Neill was pushing retirement age."

"And now he's pushing daisies," Patrice said. Her hand flew to cover her mouth. "My apologies, Eden. Retirement humor. If we don't joke about the inevitable, we risk going a little crazy."

"I understand."

"Were you visiting a friend?" Patrice asked.

"Not quite. Henrietta Egerrton," I said. "Do you know her?"

Patrice nodded. "Lovely woman. We play shuffleboard sometimes. And cards, of course. She's sharp as a tack when she's not feeling grotty."

"I'd keep my distance until her cold is gone," I said. "It's apparently highly contagious."

Patrice smiled. "Will you be coming to see her again soon? You could pay me a visit at the same time. We can play games. You were always good at those."

Gale's frown grew deeper. "Now, Mamma. Eden doesn't have time to waste on an old woman. She needs to focus on finding herself a man."

Mrs. Tanner and my mother had more in common that I cared to admit.

"I'd love to come another time," I said.

Patrice placed her palms flat against the sheet. "It's settled then. I'll expect you for another visit soon. Maybe Sassy can come with you."

"I bet she will, as soon as this outbreak passes," I said. "I promise."

CHAPTER TEN

IT WASN'T every day I got called to the mayor's office for a meeting. In fact, this was my first time ever.

"Agent Fury, we're so pleased you could join us," Mayor Wilhelmina Whitehead greeted me at the door to the conference room. At about five foot ten with deep brown eyes and a gleaming set of white teeth, the mayor cut a striking figure in her power suit. She offered her hand, but I politely declined to shake it, gesturing to my red nose.

"I'm honored to be included," I said. "I'll try to keep my germs to myself."

"That would be most appreciated," the mayor said.

"I believe you know Husbourne Crawley." The Southern transplant sat at the table in one of his trademark white linen suits.

"We're neighbors," I said. I neglected to mention that we both served on the secret supernatural council and that Husbourne was our informant on all things political in town.

A middle-aged man rose to his feet. His face was deeply tanned and his flashy, colorful suit was in sharp contrast to

Husbourne's traditional garb. "We haven't had the pleasure of an introduction. I'm Jayson Swift."

"The lawyer?" I'd never actually met the land shark, but I knew him by reputation.

He smoothed the front of his tailored suit jacket. "The one and only."

The older woman beside him laughed. "The one and only lawyer? Now there's a pipe dream." She shifted her attention to me. "I'm Edwina Melton." With her frosted blond hair and reading glasses, my guess was late sixties.

"Alex Appleton," the next man said in a gruff voice. He seemed more interested in the papers on the table in front of him than engaging with me.

"I wish our introduction was under better circumstances," Mayor Whitehead said. "We'd like to get out in front of this potential epidemic and Husbourne suggested bringing you into the fold sooner rather than later." She motioned for me to join them at the oval table.

"You do realize I'm an agent in the cybercrime division," I said. "I'm not sure how much help I can offer you."

"I'm aware of that," Mayor Whitehead said. She sat at the rounded edge of the table and slotted her fingers together. "Husbourne says you used to be in a different division. I was hoping you could lend your skills to help us identify a Ground Zero. A common denominator that might tell us how and where this bug started so we can contain it."

"For all we know, it's a really bad allergy season," Alex said. "I still think we're overreacting."

"Would you say we were overreacting if Ray Langdon had been your son?" Mayor Whitehead asked pointedly. "I seem to recall you demanding an inquisition when a tree fell in your yard."

"That neighbor of mine is a blight on society," Alex said,

clearly agitated. "I know he rigged that tree to fall. Ruined my fence on purpose."

"It was during a storm," the mayor said. "You just didn't want to pay to have it removed."

"Why should I?" Alex grumbled. "That Mother Nature can be a real bitch."

"A real powerful bitch," the mayor said. "Like me." She flashed an intimidating smile. "And this bitch's concern right now is for the residents of this town."

Alex met her steely gaze. "I've already warned you that you'll end up looking like a hysterical female. It'll cost you the next election."

Mayor Whitehead didn't flinch. "I'd rather save lives than worry about the next election. I'm not the mayor yet to come. I'm the mayor right now."

I gaped at her for an extended beat. "I don't know where you came from, but welcome to Chipping Cheddar."

The mayor looked at me and laughed. "That's right. You grew up here, didn't you? I'm a more recent transplant. Came here from Sarasota for my husband's job and loved it so much that I decided to run for mayor."

That election must've taken place when I lived in San Francisco. I'd stopped keeping abreast of town events at that point. Clara and I weren't in contact and it wasn't as though I made small talk with my family.

The door swung open and I was startled to see Chief Fox enter the room.

"Oh, fantastic," the mayor said. "I wasn't sure if you'd be able to join us. Agent Fury, have you had a chance to meet the new chief of police?"

"We've met, Mayor," the chief said, before I could answer. His gaze lingered on me longer than necessary and my body warmed in response.

"I've heard nothing but good things about both of you,"

the mayor said. "I can't help but feel that Chipping Cheddar has its best days ahead of it."

"I think its best days ended when the Puritans were overrun," Alex said. His voice was as unpleasant as his expression, as though he'd woken up in a pool of his own vomit. Based on the stories I'd heard about his penchant for alcohol, that scenario wasn't far-fetched.

"Overrun by whom?" Husbourne asked.

Alex waved a hand airily. "Everybody else. The common folk."

"Remind me not to let you write the slogan for my next campaign," the mayor said.

"As a member of the common folk," the chief began, "allow me to tell you that my deputy and I have been working on narrowing down the common locations."

"And have you identified any potential hot spots?" Mayor Whitehead asked.

"We have. One of them is a brand new business."

My heart skipped a beat. "Not Magic Beans?"

"The LeRoux place?" Husbourne added.

"Afraid so," the chief said. "The members of the band had been there right before they fell ill, including the deceased."

"Where else?" Jayson asked.

"The cafe at the marina," Chief Fox said. "The band had lunch there earlier in the week."

"How about anyone else that's sick?" I asked.

He seemed to notice my symptoms for the first time. "You caught it, Agent Fury?"

"I was at The Devil's Playground the night Ray died," I said. "I'm sure a bunch of people caught it that night."

"That's why it's hard to nail down a Ground Zero," Edwina said. "You don't know for sure whether the band members picked it up from a place or another person."

"I know someone else who might have been infected by a

patron of Magic Beans," I said. I hated to mention it because of my family's history with the LeRoux witches, but I couldn't hold my tongue.

"Who's that?" Jayson asked. All I could see in his eyes were dollar signs in connection with a potential lawsuit.

"Henrietta Egerrton is a resident at the nursing home," I said. "I think she caught it from her grandson who works in the bank next to Magic Beans. He'd been there before he went to visit her and now they're both sick."

"It's not a slam dunk, but it's a start," the mayor said. "Chief, I want you to shut the place down until further notice. See what you can find out from a health and safety inspection."

"Yes, Mayor," the chief said.

The mayor placed her phone on the table and began to tap on the screen. "I'll schedule a follow-up for two days from now and see where we're at. In the meantime, I trust that everyone here will do their best to keep the community calm and, for Pete's sake, carry antibacterial gel and a box of tissues."

"The gel won't help if it's a virus we're dealing with," Alex said.

Mayor Whitehead glared at him. "You're just a regular Contrary Mary, aren't you?"

"He's right, though," I chimed in. "If it's a viral infection, then the gel is useless." Of course, I knew for a fact the gel was useless, but I couldn't share that part.

"But that doesn't mean we shouldn't take precautions," Edwina said.

"Agent Fury, why don't you accompany Chief Fox to Magic Beans," the mayor suggested.

"Why?" I asked. "I'm sure he and Deputy Guthrie can handle it."

"I'm sure they can," the mayor said, "but a federal agent

gives the whole thing more teeth. Is that all right with you, Chief Fox?" She clearly expected an answer in the affirmative and he knew it.

"Agent Fury and I make a great team," the chief said.

I strangled a cough. "We'll just make sure we keep a safe distance. I wouldn't want to infect the chief of police."

"The sick elderly woman in the nursing home is still alive, right?" Edwina asked.

"She is," I confirmed.

"The elderly and the young are our most vulnerable residents," Mayor Whitehead said. "I don't want to close the schools, but I will if it comes to that."

I felt a surge of respect for the mayor. I knew very little about her, but I was impressed with what I'd seen so far.

"What about Cheese-chella?" Jayson asked. "The festival could end up being a safety hazard."

"Let's hope it doesn't come to that," Mayor Whitehead said.

"You're being overly dramatic," Alex scoffed. "This is an unusual cold and flu season. That's all."

I wanted desperately to put him in his place, but I couldn't. There was too much work to do, starting with Magic Beans. If Corinne LeRoux didn't hate me already, she was sure going to hate me now.

Chief Fox and I drove separately and met outside the door to Magic Beans. There were a reasonable number of guests inside. Poor Corinne was going to be deeply unhappy in about two minutes.

The chief leaned forward and sniffed me. "You smell really nice," he said.

"That's medicine for my cold. I rubbed it on my chest earlier."

His gaze shifted to my chest and back to my face. "Don't toy with me like that, Fury."

I barked a short laugh. "That screams sexy times to you?"

"What? Eucalyptus is a turn-on."

"In that case, I'd hate to see you walking around the nursing home."

His grin faded. "If this infection spreads in the nursing home, we're going to be in real trouble."

I thought of Henrietta Egerrton and Tanner's grandmother and my resolve strengthened.

I opened the door. "After you, Chief Fox."

He strode inside and I resisted the urge to run ahead and order a quick drink before we closed down the shop. Back to The Daily Grind for me.

Corinne spotted us and walked to the end of the counter to greet us. "Welcome back. Always happy to see repeat customers."

Chief Fox cleared his throat. "Miss LeRoux, I'm afraid I have to ask you to close for business."

Corinne registered shock. "Why?"

"Mayor's orders," Chief Fox said. "She wants a health and safety inspection."

"But I had one already," she argued.

"It's because of the sickness going around," I said quietly.

Corinne blinked back tears. "I don't understand. I have to close because people are getting cold and flu symptoms?"

"It's not that simple," I said. I gave her a pointed look, but she didn't seem to catch it.

Her expression crumpled. "I've only recently opened. Shutting down now will make it really hard to recover."

Chief Fox appeared sympathetic. "I understand how difficult it is to start a new business."

Corinne's gaze swept the busy shop. "I've put my heart and soul into this place, not to mention my entire savings."

"I'm sorry, Miss LeRoux," the chief said. "Truly, I am, but the health and safety of this town has to come first."

Corinne turned to face me, her dark eyes simmering with unspoken anger. "This is your family, isn't it? They're behind this."

"No, definitely not," I said with an adamant shake of my head.

Chief Fox looked at each of us, confusion etched in his handsome features. "Why would the Fury family want to hurt your business? They don't operate a rival shop."

"They're rivals all right," Corinne said. "The LeRoux family has had to put up with their bullying for far too long."

I didn't know what to say. My family did have a rivalry with the LeRoux coven, but for reasons neither of us could explain to Chief Fox. As much as I was willing to believe my family would hex a LeRoux without batting an eyelash, I didn't think they were responsible for this.

Chief Fox took a protective step in front of me. "Miss LeRoux, I assure you that we're acting in the best interest of the town and for no other purpose. There's some evidence to suggest the outbreak started in this shop. The mayor wants an inspection done ASAP."

"And my family hasn't set foot in here," I said. They wouldn't dream of it.

"No," Corinne said, her voice icy cold, "but you have."

I reeled back. "I would never sabotage you or anyone else. I love the coffee here, and that's the highest compliment. I'm a huge coffee snob. Ask anyone."

"You got the snob part right," Corinne said.

"I'm going to politely ask your customers to leave now," the chief said. "I would appreciate it if you wouldn't interfere. I don't want to have to arrest you on top of everything else."

Corinne lowered her head. "I won't, Chief. I may not like

it, but I am a law-abiding citizen." Her words were clipped and I knew she was seething. Her anger was palpable.

I waited for Chief Fox to address the customers before moving closer to the counter. "Corinne, please believe me. I'll do whatever I can to help figure this out."

Corinne's eyes met mine. "I don't even understand why you're here. You're FBM," she hissed.

"And this is a supernatural outbreak," I said softly. "The chief and the mayor don't know, so they're kind of flying blind." I paused. "We all are."

Corinne's nails clicked on the counter as she contemplated my statement. "Fine, but I want to help, too. This is my shop and I'm not leaving its fate in someone else's hands. It's taken me too long to get to this point."

A LeRoux witch offering to help a Fury? Would wonders never cease?

"If there's an opportunity for you to pitch in, I won't object," I said.

When the last customer finally vacated the building, the chief turned to address Corinne.

"I'll let you know when the inspection is," Chief Fox said.

"Thanks. Can I stay to observe?" Corinne asked. "If something in here is making people sick, I want to know what it is."

"I'm sure you can be present as a silent observer," Chief Fox said. He arched an eyebrow at me. "I'm not sure if that's possible for you."

"You don't think the inspector will let me watch?"

"I don't think you're capable of being a silent observer," he said.

Ah. Fair enough. "That's okay. I don't need to micromanage."

The chief picked up an incoming call. "I've got to go. I trust you'll lock up?"

Corinne nodded. "If I don't, I'm sure Eden won't hesitate to arrest me."

Chief Fox tipped an imaginary hat on his way out.

"He is one fine specimen," Corinne said, watching him leave. "If I weren't so annoyed about my shop, I'd be tempted to ask him out."

My head jerked toward her. "You would?"

"Is that a problem?" Corinne asked. "You're not interested from what I hear." She shrugged. "Not sure I'd mind even if you were. It's not like I owe anyone in your family any loyalty."

"No," I said. "That's true."

Corinne seemed to soften. "Listen to me. I sound like my mom." She released a gentle sigh. "There's no reason we can't be friends, Eden."

"Actually, there are a lot of reasons."

"Fine, but I'm still a fan of girl code. If you've got eyes on the chief, then say the word. I'm happy to wait to see how you two play out."

I hesitated. How could I stand in her way? I had no claim on him. He'd expressed an interest in me and I'd had to turn him down. If he decided to date Corinne LeRoux, that was his prerogative.

"I'm not interested," I said, with a heavy heart.

She smiled. "Well, you're straight-up crazy in that case, but you're a Fury, so I guess I already knew that."

CHAPTER ELEVEN

I RETURNED to the office to do some research on supernatural infections and diseases that could cause the relevant symptoms. Neville got a little too enthusiastic about the science and I tuned him out like I tended to tune out my tax preparer.

A knock on the door to the office startled both of us. I shot a quizzical look at Neville. "Answer it," I said.

His anxious gaze shifted from the door to me. "You should really answer it, O' Furious One."

"I'm going to be furious in two seconds if you don't get up and answer the door." The moment the threat left my mouth, I realized exactly who I sounded like and I felt a wave of nausea roll over me.

Neville hustled to the front of the office and peered out the window before opening the door. "It's an old woman," he called over his shoulder.

"I can hear you," a gravelly voice said.

"Uh oh," I murmured. I knew that voice.

"Can I help you?" Neville asked in a polite tone.

"I'm looking for Eden," the elderly voice said. "Her aunt told me she works here."

I'd have to have a word with Aunt Thora later. "Hello, Mrs. Paulson," I said, craning my neck to see her. "Neville, why don't you let her in?"

Neville stepped aside, giving me a curious look.

"Mrs. Paulson is my neighbor," I explained.

The old woman seemed relieved when she spotted me. "I can't believe this is where they put your office, though I suppose they figure it will cut down on travel time since so much crime happens in this section of town."

"It's not the prettiest part of Chipping Cheddar," I agreed, "but it's actually not as crime-ridden as you think." In fact, the biggest crime I'd noticed so far involved parking without putting money in the meters. I wasn't about to rat anyone out for that. It wasn't my job to generate revenue for the government.

Mrs. Paulson bustled toward me, hugging an oversized tote bag to her chest. "I need help."

"From me?"

Neville returned to his desk, but I could tell he was intently listening to our conversation.

"I think I have a virus," she said.

I inspected her closely. "You don't seem sick."

She whacked me with her bag. "Not me. My computer."

I rubbed my arm. "What makes you think I can fix a virus on your computer?"

"Because that's your job," Mrs. Paulson said.

"I'm not in IT," I said. "I'm a federal agent."

Mrs. Paulson paid me no heed. She took out her laptop and set it in front of me on the desk. "It's so slow now that it's basically useless. I can't catch up on TMZ unless I use my phone."

I opened the lid and stared at the screen. "Have you tried turning it off and on again?"

Behind me, Neville covered a laugh with a cough.

"You're supposed to be detecting cybercrime in here," Mrs. Paulson said. "There might be criminal activity on my computer. What if someone has downloaded…" She lowered her voice. "The pornography."

"It's not the title of a movie, Mrs. Paulson," I said. "It's just porn."

She smacked my arm. "Don't say it like that."

"Like the word that it is?" I asked.

"Don't give it a casual nickname, like it's your friend. People might get the wrong idea about you. Goodness knows your family already suffers from a certain reputation."

"You're right. I apologize." The fastest way to get her out of my office was to fix her computer, which I couldn't do. "Hey, Neville. I have something really official to work on. Would you mind helping Mrs. Paulson with her virus?"

"Certainly." He came over to scrutinize the laptop. I scooted over to make room for him at the desk. "Hmm. Netscape Navigator? I haven't seen that in use since…"

"Watch yourself, pudgy man," Mrs. Paulson said. "No insulting references to dates."

"Apologies. I think I can help." He tapped away on the keys and I pretended to busy myself with "official business." I couldn't risk her glimpsing my research topics.

Mrs. Paulson bent over his shoulder and watched his every move. "Is it a virus?"

"Several, actually," he said.

"It's probably the YouTube," she said. "Sometimes my son sends me a link to something he thinks is funny. I swear he must spend all his time surfing on the YouTube."

I bit back a smile. Mrs. Paulson' effort to keep up on

current vernacular was commendable, much better than Grandma's fondness for the urban dictionary.

"I need to run a few updates, if you don't mind waiting," Neville said.

"I might wander into that donut place next door," she said. "Is it safe?"

"Holes is perfectly safe," I said. "Tell Paige we sent you and she'll take good care of you."

"Excellent. Can I offer anyone a Boston cream?" she asked.

Neville perked up at the mention of his favorite pastry. "Yes, please."

She patted his head. "A young man with manners. How refreshing." She gave me a pointed look. "Your family could learn a thing or two from this gentleman."

"I'm sure he could learn a thing or two from them as well," I said.

Mrs. Paulson lifted her chin a fraction. "Nothing good, I'm sure."

She wasn't wrong there.

"Take your time, Mrs. Paulson," Neville said. "This will take more than a few minutes."

She padded out of the office with her tote bag pressed against her.

"Thanks for doing this," I said. "I don't know what my aunt was thinking sending her here."

"It's no problem," Neville said. "It sounds like she doesn't have family members close enough to offer assistance."

"I think her son lives in Atlanta with his family," I said. "Her husband died years ago."

"Maybe she's lonely," he said. "Maybe that's the reason she's so keen to stay abreast of the neighborhood business."

"Or she's just nosy and her nosiness pushed her son all the way to Atlanta," I said.

He gave me a meaningful look. "Not every family is yours, Agent Fury."

"Thank the gods." I peeked at him. "You don't say much about your family."

"There isn't much to tell. We don't engage in Fury-style shenanigans."

"And the world is a better place for it."

He chuckled. "Fighting crime in San Francisco must have seemed like a vacation for you."

I leaned back against my chair. "It was blissful. Chasing down drug traffickers was a cakewalk compared with dealing with my family. Nobody knew me there, so there was no history. No assumptions."

"People like Mrs. Paulson must make that difficult for you to outrun yourself here," Neville said.

I offered a small smile. "My family makes it impossible to outrun myself here. Wherever I go, there they are."

"I think it's there *you* are."

I thought about my threat a few minutes ago. "Yes, that, too."

Mrs. Paulson returned with a box of donuts and a bright smile. "That Paige is adorable," she said. "Can't say much for the husband, though, and what kind of name is Shia? It sounds like his parents didn't speak English."

Neville accepted the proffered box. "Your computer is all set."

"Wonderful." She pulled a change purse from her bag. "How much do I owe you?" She began to dump coins onto the desk.

"No worries, Mrs. Paulson," he said. "We're government officials. We can't accept payment."

"Oh, in that case…" She scooped the coins off the edge of the desk and back into the change purse. "More for the slot machine."

"Where do you gamble?" I asked. "The nearest casino is in Perryville."

"Buddy Watts has a…" She stopped abruptly. "Nowhere. Forget I mentioned it."

"Anything else we can help you with?" Neville asked.

I could tell her by her expression that there was and immediately wished he hadn't asked. If she wanted to put her feet on the desk and show us her bunions, I was sending her to my aunt as payback.

"Now that you mention it, I also have a problem with my cabbages, but I don't think that's something you can help me with," she said.

"Why not?" I asked.

"Because I've seen your poor excuse for a garden," she replied. "Aside from your aunt's lemon trees, it's severely lacking." Clearly, she hadn't seen my aunt's lemon trees recently.

"What seems to be the trouble with your cabbages?" I asked. It was entirely possible that my family had done something to them in retaliation for…well, for breathing in the wrong direction.

"They have holes in the leaves," Mrs. Paulson said.

"Maybe a rabbit?" I suggested.

"No, I know what rabbit bites look like," she said. "And deer can't get past the fence."

"Aunt Thora had an issue with her lemon trees recently," I said. "Maybe there's a connection. Can you describe the holes?"

"I can do better than that," she said. "I can show you pictures I took on my phone." She reached into her oversized tote bag and produced a phone. She scrolled through photos until she found the one she wanted. "Here you go."

I took the phone and examined the photos of the cabbages. "You have Netscape Navigator on your computer, but you take professional quality photos on your phone?" Sure enough, the leaves were poked full of holes. "What do you think, Neville?"

He came over to view the photos. "I agree that a rabbit isn't responsible."

"Know of anything else that leaves tiny holes in a pattern like that?" I asked.

"A pest of some sort," he said.

I hoped my aunt's insistence on having non-native plants didn't attract an invasive species.

"Would you mind sending me a copy of the picture?" I asked.

"You really think you can help me?" Mrs. Paulson asked.

"I don't know, but I'm happy to try."

She peered at me over the rim of her glasses. "Hmm. Maybe you're not like the rest of your family after all."

I couldn't resist a smile. "Thank you. Believe it or not, I consider that the highest compliment."

I arrived home from the office, feeling unwell and dispirited. I knew Corinne's interest in the chief shouldn't bother me, but it did. I tried my best to shake it off. I had far more important matters to worry about than the romantic entanglements of Chief Sawyer Fox.

My brother sat on a stool at the kitchen island, reading through a magazine.

"Looking for one of your ads?" I asked.

Anton glanced up and grimaced. "Yikes. You look like you crawled out of a swamp and then went dumpster diving."

"Gee, thanks. How are the kids feeling?" I asked.

"Ryan sleeps it off like a champ and Olivia's in good spirits, despite her annoyance at missing school," Anton said. "I don't think it's hitting her as hard. The humans are definitely worse off, from what I can tell."

"They don't have the antibodies to fight a supernatural infection," I said.

Olivia rounded the corner, looking adorable in a frilly dress, tights, a pair of my mother's high heels, and a face caked with makeup. "Aunt Eden, I've been doing makeovers."

"I can see that," I said. "I think you were beautiful before, but you're equally beautiful now."

Olivia flashed a dazzling smile. "I'm not talking about me, silly."

"Oh." I shot my brother a quizzical look as Olivia wobbled away. "Ryan?"

"Aunt Thora took him for a walk in the stroller to give him fresh air," Anton said.

Phew. At least my aunt wouldn't be teaching him how to pronounce the word "evil" in seven languages.

Olivia returned a moment later, pulling a red wagon. My hand flew to cover my mouth.

"Princess Buttercup?" I croaked.

My hellhound sat in the red wagon, wearing a pink bonnet and a ribbon with hearts tied around her neck. I'd never seen my hound look so undignified and I'd seen her at her constipated worst.

"Do you like her lipstick?" Olivia asked. "I think the color brings out her eyes."

I peered at the hellhound. Sure enough, there was a swipe of red lipstick across the hound's mouth. To her credit, Princess Buttercup seemed perfectly at ease with the whole ordeal. Apparently, once you'd been chained and left for dead outside the underworld, everything else was gravy.

"You do incredible work," Anton said. "I'm glad you've found time to be productive while you're home from school."

"Wait, there's more," Olivia said. A shrill whistle

followed and Charlemagne slithered around the corner, sporting a blue bonnet and bright pink spots of rouge on his cheeks—or whatever passed for cheeks on the face of a snake.

"Wow," I said, because that was the only word I could muster.

"Now I'll do you," Olivia announced.

I turned to see the 'you' who was standing behind me.

"She means you," Anton said.

"Oh, that's okay," I said. "I don't really do makeovers."

"That's what Mom-mom says." Olivia studied me like an artist contemplating her next creation. "I can see where I might be able to work some magic."

I glanced nervously at my brother. "You don't mean actual magic, do you?"

Olivia's eyes sparked at the suggestion. "Can I, Daddy? I promise I'll be super careful."

"It might be a good chance to practice."

I held up my hands. "Whoa. Hold on. No one is practicing magic on my face."

"Why not?" Grandma asked. "It might be an improvement."

I balked. "Where did you come from, ninja? Take off those slippers so you can't sneak up on anyone."

"Who's sneaking?" Grandma asked. "I merely wandered into my own kitchen."

"To be honest, I'm glad you're here. I need your help," I said.

"If it requires a bra or lipstick, I'm out."

I stared at her. "What would I ever need from you that requires either of those things?"

"Maybe you need me to flirt with the chief to keep him distracted while you search his office for a set of keys," Grandma said.

"This isn't *The Dukes of Hazzard*," I said. "Besides, I have an invisibility locket for that sort of thing."

Grandma eyed me curiously. "That could come in very handy around here."

"I won't be your accomplice in causing trouble," I said.

"I don't need an accomplice," Grandma said. "I'm perfectly capable of causing trouble all on my own."

"I need to know about supernatural infections and diseases," I said. "Anything that might explain what's going around here."

"And what makes you think I'd know anything about that?" Grandma asked.

"Because I know the kind of dark arts you used to practice," I said. "It wouldn't surprise me if you inflicted a few of them."

Grandma's mouth formed a thin line. "Are you accusing me of causing the sniffles?"

"It's a little worse than sniffles."

Aunt Thora returned with Ryan in the stroller, fast asleep. Anton swooped in. "I'll carry him to his crib."

"If I were responsible for this, trust me, you'd know."

"That's true," I said. "You're usually not happy until someone loses an eye." I immediately regretted putting ideas into her head.

As I feared, Grandma seemed to take the suggestion under advisement. "You know, Rita Lafferty has been sticking her nose into everyone's business lately. Maybe I should teach her a lesson."

"By removing her eye?" I asked. "How would that teach her a lesson?"

"She'd be too busy moaning about the loss of her eye to focus on anyone else." Grandma shrugged. "Problem solved."

Aunt Thora poured water into the kettle. "Make sure you take the left eye. Her right eye is the weaker one."

"Aunt Thora!" I gasped. She was normally against this sort of behavior.

My great-aunt looked at me. "She's awful, Eden. She told everyone about Geoffrey Hatch's gonorrhea, including his wife."

"Wait. How did he get an STI if his wife...?" I trailed off. "Oh."

"When I was a young girl, you'd lose a limb for less," Grandma said. "And a man could lose..."

"Grandma." I jabbed my elbow in Olivia's direction.

"What? Anatomy is important," Grandma said. "Maybe we should help Michael Bannon lose an eye, then he'd be less likely to notice damage to his car."

Olivia tugged on my sleeve. "Can I please?" She accentuated the word please until my heartstrings were properly plucked.

Aunt Thora pulled a mug from the cupboard. "I've been thinking about him."

I kneeled on the floor and let Olivia work her preschool magic on my hair and makeup. "What about him?"

"He lives alone. Has no family and people started to get sick around the time he moved in," Aunt Thora said.

Grandma appeared contemplative. "I don't sense a demon. Just a jackass."

"Could be a glamour," my mother said, making an appearance. Although there wasn't a hair out of place, I was pretty sure she'd just woken up from a nap. "Aunt Thora's right. It's something to consider." She laughed when she spotted me on the floor. "Well, that's a fabulous job, Olivia. Eden looks adorable with corkscrew curls."

Olivia smiled proudly. "Like a poodle."

"How do you explain that colorful makeup then?" my mother asked.

"She's a show poodle," Olivia corrected herself.

I peeked at my mother out of the corner of my eye. "You're loving this, aren't you?"

"I'm simply impressed with how talented my grand-daughter is," my mother said. Her statement was punctuated by a sharp sneeze. "Here I thought she'd be all demon, but there's definitely a touch of magic in her DNA, too."

Anton emerged from the hallway. "Eden, Chief Fox is here to see you."

I glanced at Princess Buttercup, still in the wagon. "One makeover and you lose the power to bark?"

"He can shoot a gun, but he can't use a phone?" Grandma muttered.

"He just wants an excuse to see her," my mother said. "An obvious tactic. I use it myself when I want to make my interest clear."

"You make your interest clear by how much cleavage you're showing," Grandma said.

"What's cleavage?" Olivia asked.

"You'll find out when you're about twelve," my mother said. "Unless you take after Aunt Eden. Then it'll be more like sixteen."

I glared as I stalked past her and went to the door. It was only when I saw the chief's expression that I remembered my current state.

"You...That's a new look," Chief Fox said, treading carefully.

"My niece is sick," I said. "She needed a project."

He burst into a smile. "I think she found one." He stuffed his hands into his pockets. "I was in the neighborhood, so I came by to update you on the health and safety report for Magic Beans."

"You have the report already?" I asked.

"Mayor Whitehead put a little pressure on some folks," he said.

That was understandable. "Wait. You were in this neighborhood?" I asked.

"Yes," Chief Fox replied. "I had to stop by your new neighbor's."

"Let me guess—Michael Bannon?"

The chief smirked. "He seems to be having trouble settling in."

"Did he complain about us?" I asked.

"He complained about a lot of things," the chief said, "including global warming, taxes, and his rheumatism."

"You should've sent Deputy Guthrie."

"Next time, I intend to." He suppressed a laugh. "I'm sorry. It's hard to take you seriously with that…" He pointed to my face.

I cocked an eyebrow. "Artwork?"

"Sure. Let's go with that." He cleared his throat. "Anyway, the preliminary report looks good."

"So nothing that would cause illness?" I asked.

"Not so far," he said. "They're going to run a few tests on samples they collected and get back to me."

"She can't reopen yet, can she?" I asked.

"Not until we're one hundred percent, but if we can rule out Magic Beans, it helps."

"Thanks for keeping me in the loop."

"That was the mayor's request." The chief reached for a strand of hair and gently tugged the curl only to watch it bounce back in place. "Next time you're doing makeovers, will you let me know?"

"So you can join in?"

He grinned. "So I can watch. Your family seems much more entertaining than television."

I stifled a groan. "You have no idea."

CHAPTER TWELVE

I WATCHED Chief Fox drive away and then hurried to the bathroom to clean off Olivia's artwork. If Magic Beans wasn't Ground Zero, then maybe it was time to investigate my new neighbor.

I slipped back out of the house before anyone noticed. I didn't want any volunteers tagging along. I walked around the cul-de-sac, pretending to be out for an evening stroll. Pretty unlikely without Princess Buttercup, but I didn't want to risk having the hellhound with me when I was trying to be discreet. I passed Mrs. Paulson's house, the home of the three Grace sisters, and a couple of others. I only slowed my pace when I came within view of Bannon's house. The lights were off and the car was gone. Perfect.

As I rounded the corner to snoop around the backyard, I caught sight of a familiar figure bent over a bush. "Grandma?"

She turned slowly toward me. "Fancy meeting you here."

"What are you doing in Mr. Bannon's bushes?"

"If I said peeing, would you believe me?"

I crossed my arms. "Nope."

Grandma tried to distance herself from the bush. "I was curious to see how he was trimming them. The shape is perfect."

"That's not even remotely plausible." I brushed past her and peered into the bush. "What did you do?" Then I saw it glimmering in the darkness. A tiny golden pouch stuffed into the base of the bush. I reached down and retrieved it. "Really, Grandma?" I didn't need to open it to know what it was.

"What's the big deal? You've met him," Grandma said. "He's awful."

"But you're even more awful," I shot back. "You've been terrorizing him."

"Rightfully so," she sniffed. "He deserves every difficult night of sleep he gets."

I opened the pouch and sniffed. "I don't know this hex."

"You wouldn't," she replied. "You never showed an interest."

"Because I don't hex anyone," I said. "Nor should you."

Grandma muttered a response that included several obscenities.

"You could just declare that I'm not the boss of you and be done with it," I said. "No need for foul language."

"Oh, now you're telling me how I can express my displeasure, too? Sheesh. What won't you criticize, Little Beatrice?"

I flinched. Was I really becoming like the rest of my family? Like *my mother*? "We're taking this pouch home."

"You can't leave now," Grandma said. "Aren't you here to investigate him?"

I shoved the pouch into my pocket. "Fine. You go home and I'll bring the pouch when I finish here."

"I can help," Grandma said.

I launched a skeptical eyebrow. "You will?"

"Sure. If he's guilty, then I'll feel free to do worse than hex him."

"You will not," I snapped. "You'll let me handle it as part of my job."

Grandma blew a raspberry. "Yeah, yeah. Your job. Is there no end to referencing it?"

I studied the back door. "You should probably go home now."

Grandma elbowed me out of the way. "And let you break in by yourself? Fat chance. I'm breaking in with you."

"Grandma, that isn't a good idea," I said. "You're not an FBM agent."

"No, but I'm not a law-abiding citizen either."

I held my hands over my ears. "You didn't just tell that to a federal agent."

"Here, I'll get us in." Before I could stop her, she touched the sliding glass door and said an incantation. The door slid open far enough that we could enter.

"You didn't use black magic, did you?"

She made a face. "For a simple unlocking spell? I think that cold must've gone to your head."

I entered the house first and immediately turned around and flicked my fingers, using a barrier spell to block Grandma from following.

Grandma took a step forward and bounced backward. "Ungrateful spawn! How dare you disrespect your elder."

"Sorry, Grandma. Can't let you break the law. Thanks for unlocking the door, though." I ignored the stream of curses hurled at me and continued deeper into the house. The layout was completely different from our house, which made sense. Michael Bannon's house was a suburban, split-level style.

At a glance, nothing seemed unusual. There still stacks of boxes pushed against the walls waiting to be unpacked. I peeked in a few random ones to see sports equipment, lesser-used kitchen items like a blender and a crockpot, and framed photographs. I pulled out one of the larger frames for a better look. A younger, tuxedo-clad Michael smiled back at me, next to a blushing bride. She was pretty, with blond hair cut just below her ears and a winning smile. The glass had a diagonal crack from one corner to the other. I wondered whether the damage had been accidental or intentional.

Carefully, I returned the frame to the box and closed the lid. The downstairs held nothing of interest, so I ventured upstairs. The living room and dining room were mostly bare. There was a weathered recliner in the living room and a television on a console table. No large flat screen on the wall like most men would have, suggesting that television wasn't his main form of entertainment.

The kitchen seemed to be in the best shape. Based on the fully stocked cupboards and variety of pots and pans, it appeared that Michael liked to cook. Well, that was one point in his favor.

I examined the spices for any sign of magical herbs. Tarragon. Salt. Pepper. Cumin. Nothing too out of the realm. I checked the drawers and noted that his junk drawer was already heaving with random items. Nice to know it was a universal thing.

I headed upstairs to the bedrooms. Two were empty so I went to the master bedroom and padded around the thick carpet. The bedroom furniture was made of a heavy cherry wood. The nicks told me it wasn't new. The well-worn bedding told me that he'd used it for a long time and that it had probably been chosen by a woman—maybe even the bride in the photograph. Why did a bachelor like Michael buy a house this big when he clearly didn't need the space? He certainly didn't strike me as the type of guy who enjoyed neighborhood life. I couldn't picture him organizing a chili bakeoff or a block party.

The bedside table only held a lamp and a book about World War II. Well, at least he and my dad would have something to discuss.

The sound of a car in the driveway sent a shiver down my spine. I dashed to the window of the bedroom to see Michael exiting the car. Oh well. I'd seen enough to be sure he was innocent. I hurried to the stairs and practically skidded all the way to the lower level to avoid being spotted when he entered the house.

"Hello?" Michael called. "Is someone here?"

Flaming bag of minotaur shit! His hearing was much better than it should be for a man his age. Whatever vitamins this guy takes, I should buy them for my father.

"I know you're in here. Is this the same ghost that's been ringing my bell?" His voice trembled with both fear and rage. He was angry that he felt scared, apparently.

I made it to the sliding glass door just as his footsteps thudded down the steps. Ha! See you later...

The door refused to budge. What in Hecate's name? I glanced outside to see Grandma standing in the backyard. She smiled and waved.

Oh no.

I placed my hand on the door and tried to use a release spell. Nothing happened. Grandma must've conjured some type of spell to prevent me from leaving.

"Hello?" Michael called again, his voice getting closer.

I gestured violently to Grandma, who cupped her hand to her ear and feigned ignorance. She was going to pay for this. Right now I was so incensed that I'd even consider killing her traitorous butt and leaving my mother to revive her.

I had to override Grandma's spell, which meant tapping into magic more potent than the kind she used. Argh! I focused my will on the door. Nothing.

I turned around to see Michael's shadow heading toward

me, so I did the only thing I could think of. I used the locket Neville made for me and turned myself invisible.

"Will you please answer me?" Michael asked. He looked more tired than angry now.

"Woooo," I said, making the first ghostly noise that sprang to mind.

He staggered backward. "Nina?"

"Michael," I said in my best spooky voice.

He dropped onto the bottom step, seemingly unafraid. "I thought it might be you. Why have you been haunting me?"

"Bad deeds." I stretched out the words as long as I could, taking care to alter my voice.

Michael covered his face in his hands. "I'm sorry. I didn't mean to lose the house. I wanted to stay there forever. It's where all the memories of us are." He started to weep.

Great Goddess. This wasn't what I expected to happen. What did I do now? Comfort him? Glide past him and sprint out the front door?

"I was able to get this house cheap," he continued. "The guy's family didn't want to put it on the market—too much of a hassle—so there wasn't much negotiation. It was the closest house I could get to ours in my price range." He sniffed. "I had to pay cash, you know. I can't get a mortgage anymore, not with my credit history."

"It's okay," I said in my spooky voice.

"It's not okay," he said. "I let you down. Even in death, I let you down."

I said the only words that I thought could possibly help —"I forgive you."

He cried openly now, his shoulders heaving. I didn't waste the opportunity to escape. I slipped past him and climbed the steps until I reached the front door. Fingers crossed that Grandma only hexed the sliding glass door.

I held my breath as I gripped the handle and the door

opened. *Thank the gods.* I slithered out the door, careful to close the door behind me so that he didn't hear the click. I bolted from the house and ran all the way home, making sure to stay invisible until I was safely in the attic.

"Michael Bannon is a regular human," I announced the next morning. "He has nothing to do with the outbreak and I'd appreciate it if you'd stop hexing him."

My mother and grandmother stared at me.

"I don't know what you mean," my mother said, lowering her eyelids.

Aunt Thora glanced up from her recipe book. "We've been hexing the new neighbor?"

"That's terrible," my mother said.

"Don't let her fool you. She knows," Grandma told me. "Who do you think put together that pouch you caught me with?"

"I'm not giving that back to you, by the way," I said. "That's your punishment for locking me inside the house."

Grandma blinked innocently. "I thought you locked yourself in there. My apologies if I misinterpreted the situation."

I folded my arms. "Nice try."

My mother remained focused on Grandma. "Why would you throw me off the broom like that after everything I do for you?"

"Like what?" Grandma scoffed.

"I put a roof over your head," my mother said. "I feed you..."

"My sister feeds me," Grandma countered. "You complain about the way I eat."

"Only because you chew so loudly," my mother said.

This argument would go to a bad place quickly if I didn't

intervene. I hustled to the pantry and pulled out the emergency spray bottle.

"Chewing only bothers you because you like to swallow your prey whole," Grandma said.

My mother shot to her feet, ready to respond. I leaped between them and spritzed each of them in the face with herb-infused water designed to calm them down. Aunt Thora had come up with the idea and prepared the tonic after the last battle between the two witches.

They both sputtered. "What are you doing?" my mother demanded. She wiped the water from her eyes.

"Um, Eden," Aunt Thora said. "That's the water I use to spray the plants in the house."

I stared at the spray bottle in my hand and swallowed hard. "Oops."

Fortunately for me, my mother and Grandma were still intent on each other. They moved from the kitchen into the living room, circling each other.

"Code Red," Aunt Thora said.

"More like Code Dead if this keeps up," I said.

Aunt Thora drummed her nails on the table. "I can't decide whether to fetch popcorn or intervene."

"Don't intervene," I warned. "It won't end well for you."

"You wouldn't kill your elder," I heard Grandma said. I moved to the threshold of the living room, debating my options.

"As if that ever stopped me before," my mother shot back.

"Nobody needs to kill anybody," I interjected. Although I wasn't about to stand between them, I was willing to object from a safe distance.

"You're already sick and old," my mother continued, a dangerous glint in her eye. "Nobody would bat an eyelid if you keeled over now."

Grandma gasped. "Are you threatening to kill me and not

revive me? And to think I let you drink from my very own breast when you were a baby."

"That's because you were too cheap to hire a wet nurse," my mother said.

"Was I breastfed?" Not a crucial question at this particular moment, but I realized I had no idea.

"Of course, sweetheart," my mother said. "Because I actually love you." She glared at Grandma.

"You only wanted an excuse to show off your boobs to anyone within range," Grandma said.

My mother glanced down at her cleavage. "Well, they are perfect specimens. They'd be in a museum if they weren't attached to my body."

Grandma waved her hand in a threatening manner. "Museum quality can be arranged."

My mother nodded toward the crystal lamp in the shape of a pineapple on the end table beside her. "Now be careful. You shoot a bolt at me now and you'll take out your favorite lamp, too."

Grandma seemed to mull it over and I thought we were in the clear until I heard the fateful words—

"Worth it."

Lightning streaked from Grandma's fingertips and zapped my mother and every object within arm's reach of her. As predicted, the lamp shattered into pieces. My mother's body reverberated from the force before a hissing noise erupted and she fell to the floor.

I moaned loudly. "You two are the worst."

"Watch it or you'll be next," Grandma said. "I don't care if you're immortal. I can still take you down for five minutes. At the very least, it'll ruin your hair." She motioned with her hand. "Not that there's far to go."

I smoothed my hair. "What are you going to do with Mom?"

Grandma contemplated the body on the rug. "I think I'll bury her and let her dig her way out. That'll teach her a lesson."

I exhaled loudly. "At least bury her with a spade so she doesn't have to ruin her nails. She just got that manicure last week."

"Yeah, but I don't like the color," Grandma said. "So it'll be like killing two birds with one lightning bolt."

"I'm not helping you," I said. "If you want to bury her, you'll have to do it without me."

"And me," Aunt Thora called. She'd wisely remained in the kitchen during the showdown.

"I'm an old woman. I'll pull a muscle," Grandma complained. "Not to mention my hernia."

"You don't have a hernia."

"I will if I have to bury her by myself."

"Then ask Anton."

"He's always working late." Grandma smiled. "I know. I'll ask your father. He'll beat a path to our door if he knows it involves burying his ex-wife."

"Don't encourage the bad blood between them," I said.

"Why not? It's fun. Besides, I guarantee you that neat-freak Sally doesn't let him play in the dirt. I'm basically doing him a favor."

I couldn't let her involve my father in this or the payback from my mother would be unrelenting.

"Fine, I'll help you, but just this once."

Grandma cackled. "I've heard that one before."

"You really shouldn't take pride in manipulating your granddaughter."

"And you really shouldn't take pride in being good all the time, yet here we are."

"That's what this is about," I said. "You want me to participate in this so that I'm an accomplice in your evil deed."

127

"No, I want you to participate so that I don't hurt myself and ruin my chance to beat Shirley at Mahjong at the senior center."

"Since when do you two play Mahjong? I thought cheating at cards was your bread and butter."

Grandma headed toward the back door. "Don't disrespect your elders, especially those with the power to bury you in the backyard."

"We all have that power."

She glanced over her shoulder. "Fine, then the ones with the willingness to bury you in the backyard."

Point taken.

I trailed behind her to the gardening shed where she retrieved two shovels and a spade.

"We're going to dig first?" I asked.

"Have to," Grandma said. "If we drag your mother out here too soon, it'll attract flies."

I grimaced at the thought of flies circling my mother's body. "Do we have to bury her?"

"No, I guess we can hang her upside down in the barn and pretend she's a bat." She chose a spot not far from Aunt Thora's suffering lemon trees and started to dig.

"Why not use magic to do this?" I asked. "Can't you enchant the shovels?"

Grandma pinned her gaze on me. "You're encouraging me to use magic?"

"It's not black magic," I said. "Besides, I'm not going to do it with you."

"Oh, I see how this works," Grandma said, leaning on the end of the shovel's handle. "You're perfectly willing to let me use my powers when it suits you, like at Bannon's house."

"It was just a suggestion. If you'd rather dig, then we'll dig."

Grandma hesitated. "Actually, it was a good idea. I just didn't think of it."

"You didn't think of it?"

She gave me a hard look. "I'm old and I forget things. What's your excuse?"

"I'm not evil?"

Grandma blew a raspberry. "That's always your excuse." She motioned for me to set down the shovel and she dropped her own.

"Do you need Aunt Thora?"

"I just killed your mother with a lightning strike, but you think I need my sister to raise a shovel?" She began an incantation and waved her hands, guiding the shovels to dig. It reminded me of the scene in *Fantasia* with the dancing buckets and broom.

Once the grave was deep enough, we returned to the house for my mother. She was exactly where we left her, except that Grandma's black cat, Candy, had fallen asleep on her scorched chest.

Grandma gazed adoringly at her familiar. "Aw, I hate to disturb her when she's curled up like that."

"We can always bury her with Mom," I said.

Grandma pointed a finger at me. "That's blasphemy." She gave a shrill whistle and the black cat stirred, barely registering our presence.

"She's not very obedient," I said.

"She's independent like me," Grandma said. "She doesn't like to be told what to do." She leaned over and tapped the cat's bottom affectionately. "Go on now before this horrid fury does something stupid."

Candy yawned and stretched before removing herself from the corpse.

I lifted my mother by the shoulders. "Grab her feet."

"Why should I grab her feet?" Grandma asked. "They smell."

"They don't smell," I said. "Take them so we can get this over with."

"Fine, if they don't smell, then you take her feet and I'll get her shoulders."

"You're ridiculous." I dropped my mother's shoulders and the back of her head hit the floor.

"That's going to leave a mark," Grandma said.

I immediately felt guilty. "Her hair will cover it."

"Not on her head, on the floor," Grandma said.

I should've known.

We carried my mother outside and heaved her into the ground. I tossed the spade on her stomach and then the enchanted shovels set to work filling in the hole. I had flash-backs to childhood, remembering similar moments. They delighted in their evil misdeeds, whereas I had always been extremely uncomfortable with them. Not much had changed.

I stood beside my mother's temporary grave and observed my grandmother's Cheshire cat grin. "You realize the payback will be ten times worse than this, don't you?"

"Not while she's sick it won't," Grandma said. "And by the time she's better, she'll have forgotten. Witches have short memories for this sort of thing."

"Probably because it happens so often," I muttered.

"What's that?" Grandma asked.

"If you find yourself killing each other on a regular basis, maybe you should reevaluate the type of relationship you have."

"I can't reevaluate it," Grandma said. "She's my daughter. It is what it is."

I smacked my forehead. "Why don't you sign some kind of peace treaty? Wave a white flag?"

Grandma looked at me like I was ready to be committed.

"You've been away too long, Eden. You forget how this family operates."

"I haven't forgotten," I said. "I was just hoping that something might have changed." A rustling sound by the gate caught my attention. "Do you hear that?" I scanned the backyard for signs of an intruder. Maybe it was the pest that had attacked the lemon trees and Mrs. Paulson's cabbages.

"I don't hear anything." I could tell from her posture that she wasn't making an effort either. She was too busy gloating over my mother's grave.

I walked around the side of the house to investigate. No sign of rabbits or anything else. "Must've been the breeze."

"Put away those shovels and I'll go inside and make us a pot of tea," Grandma said.

"Yes, because that's what serial killers do after a fresh kill. A nice cup of tea and a biscuit."

"The civilized ones, anyway," Grandma said, completely missing the point.

Reluctantly, I tidied away the shovels and followed her inside.

CHAPTER THIRTEEN

I'D BARELY MADE it out of the shower and up to the attic to get dressed when Alice swooped in front of me.

"Eden, put on lipstick," Alice said. "Hurry!"

I glanced down at my towel. "I think lipstick is pretty low on the list right now." My first priority was more vapor rub for my chest. My sleep was interrupted throughout the night by coughing fits, not to mention nightmares of my zombie mother seeking revenge.

The sound of the doorbell reverberated throughout the house. "Who is it?"

"Get dressed," Alice urged. When I reached for an orange top, her ghostly hand tried to smack my arm away. "Not that one. It isn't feminine enough."

"Listen, Alice. I already have a mother with old-fashioned ideas about fashion…" Despite my objection, I found myself putting on a cobalt blue top with an alluring V-neck and jeans. My hair would have to air dry.

Grandma intercepted me as I came down from the attic. "It's your boyfriend again. He must be really hard up for a date. Don't take him to make out in the barn unless you want to explain the fresh grave out back."

I gulped. Chief Fox was here and my mother was buried in the backyard. Great.

Princess Buttercup accompanied me to the front door, zigzagging down the hallway with exuberance.

"Hi," I said, forcing a bright smile as I opened the door. My smile faded when I noticed Mrs. Paulson on the porch behind him. "Is everything okay? Mrs. Paulson, are you having more computer problems?"

Mrs. Paulson ignored me. "Go on," she urged.

Chief Fox pinned me with a solemn gaze. "Sorry to bother you, Agent Fury, but your neighbor is concerned about recent activity in your garden and asked me to check things out."

"Oh, the invasive species?" I asked. "Aunt Thora has been struggling with her lemon trees…"

"Not the insects," he interjected.

"They buried a body," Mrs. Paulson blurted. "I saw it with my own four eyes." She tapped her glasses.

Chief Fox offered a rueful smile. "I've explained to Mrs. Paulson that she was mistaken, that a federal agent would not be covering up a murder by hiding a dead body in her own backyard, but Mrs. Paulson seems convinced."

"I don't need him mansplaining what I think I saw." Mrs. Paulson nudged him out of the way to confront me. "I came over here to thank you for helping me with my computer. I even brought muffins."

"You baked muffins for me?"

"No, I bought them at the grocery store, but still." She gestured toward the back of the house. "I heard voices, so I went around back and saw you and your grandmother with a shovel."

"Well, of course you did, Mrs. Paulson," I said sweetly. "We were gardening."

"You were digging and burying," she argued.

Although I maintained a calm exterior, my insides were churning. How would I explain this to Chief Fox? I had to think of a way to get rid of both of them.

"That's how you plant things, Mrs. Paulson. You dig and bury the roots."

"Don't lecture me on gardening, young lady," Mrs. Paulson said. If she had a cane, she would've hit me with it.

"How rude of me to leave you standing on the porch," I said. "Why don't you come in and we can discuss whatever you think you saw?"

Mrs. Paulson fixated on Princess Buttercup. "Not until you call off your Rottweiler."

"She's a Great Dane," I said. Sort of.

"Princess Buttercup wouldn't hurt a fly," Chief Fox said. He reached forward and rubbed the hound's head. "See?"

Grandma appeared behind me. "I thought I heard voices. Where are your manners, Eden? Invite them in. Who would like tea?"

Uh oh. I didn't trust that offer for a second. She might as well have offered them a nap in bed with the horse's head already on the pillow next to the mint.

"Nobody wants tea, Esther," Mrs. Paulson said. "The chief is here to investigate a murder."

Grandma wore an innocent expression. "Who died?"

"Well, not the two of you, clearly," Mrs. Paulson said.

Grandma didn't miss a beat. "Please come on in so we can figure this out in a civilized manner."

"You're taking this very well for someone being accused of burying a dead body in your yard," the chief said.

Grandma waved a hand. "Please. If I had a nickel for

every time I've been accused of a criminal act, I'd be retired by now."

"Um, you *are* retired, Grandma," I said. Not the best analogy.

Grandma laughed awkwardly. "So I am." She crooked a finger for them to follow her. "The water's already boiled."

Mrs. Paulson took a hesitant step into the house. I could see her mentally assessing the interior as she walked.

"Your house is much bigger than mine," Mrs. Paulson said.

"I suppose we're responsible for that, too," Grandma said, a trace of bitterness seeping out.

"It's because this is the original farmhouse," I interjected. "All the land on the cul-de-sac originally belonged to the Wentworth family."

Mrs. Paulson peeked in every doorway on our way to the kitchen. "And then your parents divorced and your father built that monstrosity on your property."

"They split the property in half as part of the divorce settlement," I said. Not that it was any of her business.

Chief Fox leaned down and murmured in my ear, "Sorry about this. She was adamant."

"It's okay," I said. At least I hoped it was. I had no idea how Grandma intended to handle this. I prayed to the gods that it didn't involve another dead body.

Aunt Thora stood at the counter, assembling teacups. "What a nice surprise to have unexpected visitors."

Mrs. Paulson's gaze darted around the house. "Where's Mrs. Fury?"

"Running errands," I said quickly.

"I didn't see her leave," Mrs. Paulson said.

Grandma frowned. "I didn't realize we had our own personal security system installed next door. How convenient."

I shot her a warning glance. We had to play nice or we risked agitating Mrs. Paulson even further.

"Tea?" Aunt Thora offered.

"Not yet," Mrs. Paulson said. "First, I want to show Chief Fox the backyard where I saw the grave."

He looked at me. "You don't mind, do you?"

"This way," I said. Princess Buttercup ran as soon as I opened the back door. Unfortunately, she made a beeline for the fresh mound of dirt and began to sniff around.

"See!" Mrs. Paulson pointed.

"I buried her bone," I said. "It's one of her favorite games. She likes to be the one to dig it up."

"She's lying," Mrs. Paulson said

Chief Fox seemed torn between wanting to allay the old woman's fears and wanting to throttle her.

"I wouldn't suggest trying to take her bone away," I said. "She's sweet, but she's also very territorial."

"Princess Buttercup likes me," Chief Fox said. "Why don't I just dig it up real quick and we can lay Mrs. Paulson's fears to rest? Is there a shovel around?"

My pulse began to race.

"The tea will get cold," Aunt Thora said. "Can we at least leave the digging until afterward?"

"In certain ancient cultures, they'd string you up by your toenails for refusing hospitality," Grandma said.

"Good thing we're not part of an ancient culture then, isn't it?" I said. I didn't trust Grandma not to do *something* to Mrs. Paulson's toenails in retaliation.

"I should mention I have homemade oatmeal raisin cookies," Aunt Thora added. That was news to me. I suspected there was a quick spell involved.

"My favorite," the chief said. He turned toward the house and I relaxed slightly.

Mrs. Paulson remained rooted outside. "I'm not going

back in there." She looked at the chief. "You can't trust them, Chief. They're evil. You haven't lived here long enough to know better."

Chief Fox chuckled. "Now, Mrs. Paulson, let's not be rude. They're offering us hospitality."

"Is this because you're from Iowa?" Mrs. Paulson asked. "Because this is Maryland. We don't have to be polite here."

"Clearly," Grandma muttered.

"I'm going inside for a cup of tea and a cookie," Chief Fox said. "I suggest you join us."

Mrs. Paulson gave us a sharp look. "Fine, but keep that gun handy, Chief, in case you need to defend yourself."

His brow lifted. "You ladies own firearms?"

"Not us," Grandma said. "We've got a perfectly good guard dog."

Chief Fox grinned as he glanced at Princess Buttercup. "Fair enough."

We reentered the house and Aunt Thora immediately poured the tea. Although I had no idea which spell they planned to use, I had no doubt that the tea was laced with magic.

"I think I hear Ryan waking up," I said. "Let me check on him."

"I'll help," Grandma said. "He's been fussy since he's been sick."

Grandma and I hurried to the bedroom where Ryan was still fast asleep. I closed the door behind us.

"Please don't hurt them," I whispered.

"Relax, Jenny B. Goode," she said. "We're not foolish enough to hurt the chief of police. It's only a memory spell. No black magic."

"What kind of memory spell?" I needed Chief Fox to remember the current investigation, not to mention that the selfish part of me wanted him to remember our lighthouse lip-lock.

"It's targeted," Grandma said. "Only erases the last hour."

Phew. "Thank you," I said. "Although if it weren't for your zap-happy finger, we wouldn't be in this mess."

"Blame your mother. She started it."

"I will, once you bring her back to life." I arched out of the bedroom and back into the kitchen where everyone sat at the table with their tea.

"This is such an interesting flavor," Chief Fox said. "What did you say is in it? I've already forgotten."

"Special recipe from my mother," Aunt Thora said. "It's been handed down for generations."

"All the best recipes are," Mrs. Paulson said. "I have a rhubarb pie recipe from my grandmother that knows no equal." She swallowed a mouthful of tea.

"I'd love to try to make it," Aunt Thora said.

"Pffft. Fat chance. I don't share that with anyone. You'd have to pry the recipe from my cold, dead hands." She stopped. "Speaking of dead..." She stopped and wrinkled her nose. "Dead what?"

"I think you were talking about your garden," I said.

Chief Fox's expression turned blank. "Why did I come here then?"

"Mrs. Paulson asked you to look at her cabbages and then we showed you the lemon trees," I said.

"Did we figure out what ate my cabbage leaves?" Mrs. Paulson asked.

"Some kind of pest," I said.

"I have an organic preventative," Aunt Thora said. "I can give you a mixture along with the ingredients so you can make it yourself. To be fair, it hasn't worked for my lemon trees, but it might help your cabbages."

Mrs. Paulson nodded. "That would be nice, thank you."

Chief Fox scraped back his chair. "As enjoyable as this has been, I should probably get back home and take Achilles for a walk."

"I should go, too," Mrs. Paulson said.

Aunt Thora disappeared into the pantry and emerged with a jar and a note. "Here you are, Mrs. Paulson."

I walked the two of them to the door to say our goodbyes. Unsurprisingly, Chief Fox lingered on the front porch after Mrs. Paulson had gone.

"I haven't gotten the final report for Magic Beans yet," he said. "We closed down the cafe, too. The inspection was done this morning. I'll let you know when I find out more."

"Thanks."

"How are you feeling?" Chief Fox asked. "You look a little better."

"Still congested, but still alive." I winced. Under any other circumstances, it would've been an acceptable statement. Right now, it seemed like I was gloating.

"No new symptoms?" the chief asked. "The hospital has reported more digestive cases coming in."

"You don't need to worry about me," I said. "I have a strong constitution. I can eat Chinese food for days with no repercussions." Ugh. Gross. Why did I share that?

His brow creased. "Good to know." He hooked his thumb in the direction of Mrs. Paulson's house. "I'm sorry about that whole thing. I think she might be lonely and looking for reasons to interact."

"I wish she was willing to spend time at the senior center," I said. "She's not interested in that kind of socializing, though."

"That was nice of you to use your FBI skills to fix her computer," the chief said.

"Yep, that was all me and my tech skills," I lied.

He grinned. "Your hair looks good wet. You must've just finished your shower when we got here, huh?"

"Save your dirty thoughts for the drive home." I gave him a gentle shove off the front porch and he laughed.

"I'll text you later with an update."

"On the investigation, not your dirty thoughts." I kept my smile in place until he returned his car. Slowly, I closed the door and leaned against it, my heart pounding.

"Now can we please resurrect my mother?"

CHAPTER FOURTEEN

CHOPHOUSE IS one of the best restaurants in Chipping Cheddar, so I considered it a perk to take Paul Pidcock's place on the supernatural council, knowing I'd get to eat here once a month. Not that I needed an excuse. My cousin Rafael owns the highly regarded restaurant and also serves as its chef.

I threaded my way through the chic decor until I reached the small room at the back of the restaurant that was normally reserved for private parties. Aggie Grace was already seated at the round table, along with Adele LeRoux, Corinne's grandmother, Husbourne, and Hugh Phelps.

"Now that we're all here, let's get straight to New Business," Adele said.

Aggie raised a bony finger. "Could we order appetizers first? My mouth has been watering for the roasted brussels sprouts all day. Nobody makes them like Rafael."

The door burst open and my cousin stood framed in the doorway. "Did someone summon the kitchen wizard?"

"Good evening, Rafael," Aggie said. "Our usual drinks and the sprouts, please."

"What's on the sprouts?" Hugh asked. "I'm pretty particular when it comes to vegetables."

"As am I," Rafael replied.

"They're topped with cheese," Husbourne said. "Lip-smacking delicious."

Rafael tensed. "The sprouts are not *topped with cheese*, as you so inelegantly put it, white wizard."

"This is all very confusing," Hugh said. "Can we get back to solving society's problems after we've ordered the cheese sprouts? I'm ravenous."

Rafael bristled. "My sprouts are exquisitely prepared. They are not diner fries."

"Don't be quick to knock those," Hugh said. "Gouda Nuff serves excellent cheese fries."

Rafael pulled a face. "Please do not compare my masterpiece with what passes for food there. One does not simply chuck these sprouts into an oven and roast them. First, they are finely trimmed and dusted with a mixture of parmesan, olive oil, garlic, as well as my own secret seasoning."

"No one doubts your culinary genius," Adele said. "Hugh's a finicky eater, that's all."

"I thought werewolves ate everything," I said.

"Not their greens, apparently," Aggie said wryly.

Rafael gave a slight bow and exited the room.

"Now, can we please begin?" Adele asked. "This outbreak is a huge concern for everybody, especially with Cheese-chella coming up. The mayor's worried she might have to cancel."

"You can't cancel the cheese festival," Aggie said. "It's one of the highlights of the year." The Grace sister looked at me, her wrinkled lips compressing. "What can you tell us, Eden?"

"I know it's supernatural in nature," I said. "Beyond that, I don't know at this point. It also seems to be affecting humans disproportionately. Their symptoms are more severe. We're getting by with cold symptoms. Humans are getting hit with flu symptoms and digestive problems."

"And death," Aggie added. "Don't forget Ray Langdon."

"I haven't," I said. "I'm worried about the nursing home right now. There's one case I'm aware of, but hopefully, it's contained."

Hugh snarled. "We need to get this under control and fast. I'm trying to plan my wedding, but both the caterer and the justice of the peace have fallen ill. I can't afford any more setbacks."

Adele looked at him askance. "Your wedding? Since when?"

"Since the arrival of my intended," Hugh said. "That supernatural fog delayed the shipment of my bride and I'm not about to let another occurrence set us back even further."

Aggie coughed. "I'm sorry. Did you say shipment?"

Hugh stiffened. "Yes. She's a mail-order bride."

Everyone exchanged curious looks—except me, because I already knew all about her.

"I didn't realize this sort of thing was back in fashion," Adele said.

"I don't know that it's in fashion as much as it's a necessity," Hugh replied.

I suppressed a laugh.

"You consider a mail-order bride a necessity?" Aggie asked.

"The survival of the pack is paramount," Hugh said. "I need to start producing pups or my future alpha status will be called into question."

"Heavens, no. Not your manhood." Aggie drew back, hand on heart.

Hugh didn't seem to grasp her sarcasm. "Exactly. The sooner I can start a family of my own, the better off I'll be."

"I'm sorry about your delayed wedding," I said. "Hopefully, everything will get back to normal soon." What was I saying? Nothing ever seemed normal in Chipping Cheddar—and yet normal was all I ever wanted.

Rafael entered the room with our round of Fairy Dust and the fancy sprouts. I swirled the glass of golden liquid. I couldn't smell the sweet aroma thanks to my congestion. Hopefully, my taste buds were still in working order because this drink was the closest I'd ever get to nectar.

"So you're telling me we have no idea whether this supernatural outbreak is due to a demon or something else entirely," Aggie said.

"What about that new fella on our street?" Husbourne asked. "Didn't his move into Dudley's house coincide with the first few cases?"

"Michael Bannon is unpleasant, but he's not a harbinger of disease," I said. "I checked him out. He's human."

"He wouldn't be the first human to dabble in magic he doesn't understand," Husbourne said.

"When I say I checked him out, I *might* have entered his house and looked around. He's clean."

Hugh gave me an admiring glance. "I like your style, Fury."

"Just be sure to keep her *style* from Mayor Whitehead's ears," Adele said. "As far as she knows, Eden isn't a field agent."

Excitement bubbled to the surface at the mention of the mayor. "Tell me more about Mayor Whitehead," I said. "Is she really as cool as she seems?"

"I fully admit I was skeptical at first," Husbourne admitted, "but she won me over. She's smart and capable and she cares about everybody, from the janitor at the senior center to the director of the hospital. What she doesn't know, she's willing to learn."

"How did we ever elect someone like that?" I asked, somewhat amazed.

"I think we got lucky," Husbourne said. "She ran against Lawrence Beech. His wife caught him cheating during the election and she made it her personal crusade to see that her husband lost the election. His wife basically handed Mayor Whitehead the race on a silver platter."

I wrinkled my nose at the thought of Lawrence Beech as mayor of Chipping Cheddar. He'd been the girls' soccer coach when I was in high school and I still remember the way he leered at everyone in their skimpy uniforms. "Are they divorced now?"

"Sure are," Husbourne said. "Janine took her half of their small fortune and relocated to Palm Beach, where she met a wonderful gentleman at the country club and they got married last year."

"You really do keep tabs on everyone, don't you?" I asked.

He shrugged. "I consider it my sworn duty."

Hugh pushed the plate of brussels sprouts toward me. "You haven't tried one yet."

I speared one with my fork and popped it into my mouth. Yep, my taste buds were fully functional. "I don't even like sprouts and these are divine."

"I hope for Rafael's sake that Chophouse isn't next on the mayor's list to close," Aggie said. "I heard the cafe at the marina is closed now."

"And Corinne's new place," Husbourne added.

I shot Adele a guilty look. Even though it wasn't my fault, I felt responsible for the closure of Magic Beans.

Adele folded her hands on the table. "She's worked very hard. It's a shame her business has gotten tangled up in this mess."

Husbourne gave her arm a reassuring pat. "She'll be up and running again soon. My friend Byron considers himself quite the espresso aficionado and he thinks Magic Beans' beans are out of this world."

"Thank you kindly," Adele said. "I'll be sure to pass that along. It'll cheer her up a bit."

I swallowed another sprout, nearly choking in the process. "What did you say, Husbourne?"

"Come now, Eden," Adele said. "Corinne told me you've been in there a few times because you were so impressed."

I waved my hand. "No, no, not that. About the beans."

Husbourne frowned. "You mean that Byron thinks they're out of this world?"

"Yes, that's it." I shot to my feet. "Adele, could you please call Corinne and ask her to meet me at the coffee shop?"

"But we haven't finished the meeting yet," Aggie said.

"Send me a copy of the minutes," I said. "Right now, I've got an inspection to do."

I stared at the shipment on the floor of the Magic Beans stockroom. "I can't believe I didn't think of this."

"The inspector took bean samples," Corinne said. "He didn't find anything wrong with them."

"He wouldn't," I said. "These coffee beans are from Otherworld."

Corinne jerked. "What? What makes you say that?"

I pointed to the winged monkey logo on the sack. "Those are Potis beans, Sally's favorite brand. She complains that she can't get anything close to it in the human world." Sally complained so often that it was a minor marvel I managed to remember this one.

Corinne bent over to examine the jute sack of coffee beans. "You're sure?"

"Positive," I said. "So much for your claims of being a law-abiding citizen." Supernaturals knew that it was illegal to important products like coffee beans from Otherworld. I was actually disappointed. I wanted to believe Corinne was above that sort of thing.

Corinne hugged herself. "I didn't know, Eden."

"How could you not know where your coffee beans were coming from? You're the sole owner."

"I used a distributor," Corinne said. "Someone my mom knows."

Ah. That explained it. Of the three LeRoux witches, Rosalie was the one you had to watch out for. Although she wasn't at my family's level, her hands weren't exactly clean.

"Do you think the beans are making people sick?" Corinne asked. She opened a sack and scooped a handful of beans to study them.

"I doubt it," I said. "We'd have a lot more cases, and they'd be more digestive in nature. We're dealing with a mixed bag of symptoms."

"If it's not the beans, then what is it?" Corinne asked.

Aunt Thora's beloved lemon trees sprang to mind, and Mrs. Paulson's cabbages. "It's a pest."

Corinne cut a glance at me. "Like a rat?"

"More like a supernatural insect that hitched a ride here in one of these bags," I replied. "It's small enough to bite supernaturals without being seen."

"And it's invisible to humans anyway," Corinne said, understanding. "How did I not get bitten?"

"Why do mosquitos only bite certain people in a group?" I said. "Insects are drawn to certain food sources for a variety of reasons. They love my brother Anton's blood because he loves beer."

Corinne shifted her attention back to the shipment. "So one bug has managed to infect all these residents?"

"The bug has infected some people and then we've spread the rest ourselves with whatever germs the insect injected us with. That explains the different symptoms, too."

"As well as the severity," Corinne said. "I bet Ray Langdon was bitten." Her brow creased. "Oh, Goddess. I bet he was bitten here in my shop." She covered her mouth.

"It's not your fault, Corinne. You didn't know."

"This is my shop," Corinne said. "I'm responsible for everything that happens here." She resealed the sack. "What do I do with all these beans?"

"Let's not worry about that right now," I said. "First, Neville and I need to do a little research and figure out exactly what we're dealing with." Only then could we determine how to stop it.

"I'll help you," Corinne offered. "I want to make it right."

"You can help me by giving me the name of your distributor," I said. I'd pass that straight over to FBM headquarters. "Neville and I will handle the rest."

Corinne blinked back tears. "What if I reopen and the shop fails because the coffee isn't good anymore?"

To be fair, I shared her concern, but I couldn't let my caffeine needs get in the way of the investigation.

"One crisis at a time, Corinne," I said.

I sat beneath my sun lamp, typing away on the keyboard in my office.

"Hunting for a supernatural bug in Chipping Cheddar is like searching for a fang at a vampire convention," I complained. "What am I supposed to do? Walk around with a magnifying glass like those cartoon detectives?"

"It would make you look more sleuth-y," Neville said.

"I don't need to look sleuth-y," I said, agitated. "I'm an FBM agent. I have a badge and everything."

"Try a sloth demon," Neville said from his adjacent desk.

I craned my neck to look at him. "Why do you keep doing that?" I asked. "If you know a name, then you look it up."

"I'm coming up with options faster than I can type them," Neville said. "I'm trying to multi-task."

"I don't think it counts as multi-tasking when you give someone else the work. That's just division of labor." I typed in 'sloth demon' and grimaced. "How about you research the really unattractive ones?" I read the brief summary and immediately dismissed it. "This one leaves a trail of slime, so he's out. We should include all the details that we know as a filter."

"You're quite right," Neville said.

"The key factor is probably that it's drawn to coffee beans," I said.

"Or perhaps it's native to the area where the beans are sourced in Otherworld," Neville said.

"Good point." I added the features and qualities I was looking for and scanned the results. Each one was uglier than the last. "I feel like I'm on the worst dating app ever."

Neville chuckled. "These creatures are not Instagram-ready, are they?"

"No filter in the world can help this one." I studied the description. "A saliva demon. Ugh, it actually lives on others' saliva." I wrinkled my nose in disgust. "Gross." At least I could move on from that one.

"I see your saliva demon and raise you one better. This one leaves rotting skin behind," Neville said. He inclined his head toward his computer screen.

"Whose skin?" I asked. "His or someone else's?"

"Does it matter?"

"Fair enough." I returned my focus to the search results and my heart started to pound. "Neville…"

"Yes, m'lady?"

"This isn't Downton Abbey."

Neville heaved a sigh. "If only."

"I think I found our demon." I tapped my screen and Neville came over to read the description.

"A borer demon," he said, frowning. "I'm not familiar with that one."

"Look at those eyes," I said. They were huge, black, and round.

"Zoom in on those mandibles," Neville said, enthralled. "They're impressive."

"I didn't peg you for a mandible guy," I joked.

Neville scrutinized the description. "It loves coffee beans and leaves microscopic bites that can cause illness." He clapped his hands together once. "Great Nefertiti! We're in business."

I twisted to look at him. "Nefertiti? That's your go-to?"

"She was a remarkable woman of her time," Neville said. "Anyone who successfully spearheads a religious revolution has earned my respect, regardless of whether I agree with the worship of a sun god."

I turned back to the screen. "I'll bear that in mind. Now, the million dollar question—how can we catch a borer demon and send it back to Otherworld?"

"I'm not sure that we can."

"What do you mean? There has to be a way to get rid of it."

"Get rid of it, yes," Neville said. "But I don't think we'll be able to send it back to Otherworld alive." He pointed to the screen. "*That* is the only surefire method."

I quickly reviewed the final paragraph. "We have to smash it with a hammer?"

"Not just any hammer," Neville said. "That specific hammer. It's designed to penetrate the borer demon's protective shell."

"Too bad it isn't Thor's hammer," I said.

Neville glanced at me. "You have access to such a treasure?"

"No, but I'd like access to his hammer," I said. "Thor's hot."

Neville snorted. "Unfortunately, this hammer is not connected to the thunder god."

"The Hemiptera Hammer," I read aloud. "A picture of the weapon would be nice. How are we supposed to find it?" I continued to read. "Oh, crap. We don't have time to send a team to the deepest region of Otherworld. That'll take too long."

"We'll have to try to summon it," Neville said. "That's the fastest way."

"Do you think we'll be able to?"

"I don't see any reason we shouldn't be able to call it forth."

I sat quietly for a moment, wondering how much magic I'd have to use. Neville placed a hand on my shoulder.

"I don't think it should trigger any new fury powers," he said. "It's only a summoning spell."

"How did you know that's what I was thinking?"

He patted my shoulder once before withdrawing his hand. "It's always at the forefront of your mind. Well, that and Chief Fox."

"Hey! Since when are you some kind of psychic wizard?"

"All that's required is for someone to spend time with you to see what's important to you," he said.

"Well, you're also someone I don't have to lie to," I said. "That helps."

Neville returned to his desk. "I can see how it would."

"At least this is one part of the lie that's true," I said.

"What is?"

"I'm using a computer to do my job," I said. "Not quite ransomware or porn, but it's close enough."

"Technology plays a role in most jobs, Agent Fury. It's good to learn."

I printed the information about the borer demon for reference. "This is a huge breakthrough, Neville," I said. Except for the part about summoning the mystical hammer. That could prove to be a challenge.

"The FBM is fortunate to have you," Neville said.

"Oh, stop," I said. "I haven't even done anything yet."

"But you will," Neville said, with an air of confidence. "And now that we've identified the demon, I can start working on a potion to treat the sick. We'll have to figure out a way to administer it to the affected human population, but I'm sure Verity can help with that."

"You can make potions?" I asked. "I thought you were more mechanical than medical."

"I'm a wizard, Agent Fury," he said. "My skills are multi-faceted."

I offered Neville a grateful smile. "How about that? I guess I'm not the only one the FBM is fortunate to have."

Neville suppressed a smile. "Indeed."

CHAPTER FIFTEEN

"Can't you just kill it?" Aunt Thora asked with a shudder.

I'd driven straight home to gather the ingredients necessary to summon the hammer. My family had pounced on me with questions once I'd revealed my discovery.

My mother rolled her eyes. "You know our Eden. Even as a kid, she had a no-kill policy for spiders and other insects. If she found one in the house, she had that jar…"

"Oh, I remember that," Grandma said. "She painted 'shelter in place' on the side and would use it to carry them safely to the garden."

My mother snorted. "Remember when she rallied against our use of pesticide potion on the garden? She staged a protest in front of it."

Grandma cackled. "But then we just sprayed the potion on both of them."

"Yes," I said stiffly. "That was so hilarious."

"Hey, it got rid of the lice we didn't even know you had," my mother said. "Consider it a favor."

"I also thought it was particularly funny when you turned me into a cricket," I said.

My mother smacked her hand on the table, laughing. "That's because you talked nonstop. Chirp, chirp."

"You could have at least turned me into a bird so I could fly away from here," I said.

"Are you sulking?" Grandma asked. "She's sulking, Beatrice."

"I see that." My mother seemed to find it amusing.

"I think we should've left you buried for longer," I said.

My mother glowered in response. "Tell us what you need, Cricket Dundee and we'll help you gather the materials, if only to destroy this menace once and for all."

"No, thanks. Knowing you, you'll throw in a poison plant."

"Do you think I want this borer demon on the loose?" my mother asked. "Once I drink the potion, I don't want to worry about reinfection."

"And I'm tired of cleaning up after sick kids," Grandma said. "Let us help already."

"Fine," I huffed, and told them what I needed.

An hour later, Neville and I were in the attic with Alice guarding the entrance in case my family decided to be nosy. The wizard and I sat cross-legged on the perimeter of the circle, along with thirteen glowing candles and a bowl of magic herbs.

I pulled out my phone, tapped the screen, and sat it on the floor in front of me.

"Agent Fury?"

The calming sounds of the ocean rolled over us. "It'll help us focus," I said. "I learned it in yoga class."

"I didn't realize you were a yogi."

"I'm more like the bear." I'd never met a picnic basket I didn't like. I closed my eyes and tried to de-clutter my brain.

"Join hands, Agent Fury." Neville reached forward and clasped my hands.

"White Witch, hear our call," I said. "We request from thee the Hemiptera Hammer, so that we may protect the children of Adam and Eve, as well as Otherworld's progeny."

A slight breeze tickled my nose. I kept my eyes closed and maintained my focus.

"Give us the strength to defeat this deadly foe. We beseech thee."

The air shifted and I heard a thump.

"Did it work?" I opened my eyes and peered at the center of the circle.

"Well, it's a hammer," Neville said. He crawled forward and lifted the object from the floor, holding it up for inspection.

"That's just a DeWalt," I said.

"Maybe so," Neville said, "but it is an excellent hammer." He wielded it like a weapon.

"Put it aside, Neville. It's not our mystical weapon."

"How can you be certain?"

"Because you generally can't buy one in aisle five at the hardware store." I took a deep breath and reentered myself. "Let's try again."

We performed the same incantation one more time. I tried to alter my inflections in case that was the issue. I heard a thud and popped open one eye to see a croquet mallet.

"This is ridiculous," I said. "Something must be interfering with the summoning spell."

"I can go over the information again," Neville said. "It's possible I missed a small detail that would impact our choice of summoning spell."

"There weren't enough details," I said. "That's the problem."

"Perhaps we should request the assistance of your family," he said.

"No," I said sharply. "Definitely not. I don't need any more fury traits. Immortality is quite enough."

Neville regarded me. "You say that as though it's a bad thing. Supernaturals have killed for much less."

"Who wants to live forever?" I asked. "Watch everyone you love wither and die?" I shook my head. "Not me, thanks."

He drummed his fingers on the floor in a nervous gesture. "I guess that's one more reason not to get involved with Chief Fox."

I snapped to attention. "What?"

"Now that you're immortal, you'll outlive him."

My chest tightened at the thought. "Not like I needed another reason, but yeah." I pushed the thought of the handsome police chief from my mind. Now wasn't the time for swooning or lamenting. I had work to do. "We need to focus, Neville."

"I don't think the ocean waves are working," he said.

I rose to my feet. "I think I need a stronger pose." I clapped my hands over my head and put my foot on my leg, mimicking Mrs. Marr's tree pose.

"That's…unorthodox," Neville said. He stood and copied me. "You think this might help?"

"It's a position of strength," I said. "Can't hurt to try."

We closed our eyes and focused our will.

"By the power of the gods, I summon thee, O' mighty Hemiptera Hammer," I said. "We call upon your aid in this time of strife." It was like the Bat signal, but for an ancient weapon instead of a gravelly-voiced guy in tights.

The candles flickered as a cold wind rushed through the attic. In the middle of the circle, an object began to take shape. I reached for it, but my hand sliced through the air.

"It isn't corporeal yet," Neville said in a hushed tone. "Keep concentrating."

I resumed my position and willed the hammer into existence. My whole body strained from the effort. My siphoning magic was the worst offender when it came to draining me of energy, but a spell like this came a close second.

I peeked one eye open to see the object begin to glow with an orange light.

"This is definitely it," I said, growing excited. "The description mentions an orange light."

Neville studied at the object. "I believe you're right, Agent Fury."

Slowly, I inched closer to examine it. "This has to be it. You know, a picture would really be useful in a situation like this."

"I'll write a strongly worded letter," Neville said, completely sincere.

"Who would call that a hammer?" I asked, unable to disguise my irritation. "It's more like a fat sickle."

"Or a chunky scythe," Neville added.

I laughed. "That would be a good name for a band." I could picture Chunky Scythe emblazoned on T-shirts with the image in the background. Better than Ghost of Billy Crystal.

I plucked the hammer from the air and wielded it like a sword. "I hope this does the trick."

Neville held out his hand. "May I?"

I dropped it into his hand and he nearly fell to the ground from the weight of it. "It rather *is* like Thor's hammer." He didn't dare try to recover it.

I swept the hammer off the floor. "I guess I'm worthy Thor in this scenario."

Neville brightened. "Does that mean I get to be Loki? He is a favorite of mine."

"He's a favorite of everybody's," I said. "No time for tricks, though. We need to track this demon so I can get rid of it once and for all."

"According to the information, the demon likes to hide in marshes."

"Then I guess we should start with the marshes in town."

"I've already taken the liberty of identifying them on the map," Neville said. "There are a few, given our proximity to the river and the bay."

"The biggest one is near Cheddar Gorge," I said. "We'll try there first." It was both rural and large enough to hide a stealthy borer demon.

"Let me assemble a few items first," Neville said. "It can't hurt to have backup."

I hefted the weapon in my hand. "I hate to say it, Neville, but somebody has to."

He shot me a quizzical look. "Say what, Agent Fury?"

I looked him dead in the eye. "It's hammer time."

"I knew I should've worn boots," I said. The squelching and squirting of the mud beneath our feet seemed relentless. I had to be sure to go straight home for a shower and not stop at my dad's house for any reason. Sally would stick her fangs in me if I tracked mud like this in their house.

"Any sign of activity?" Neville asked. His giant magnifying glass made his one eye look comically enormous.

"Only rapid eye movement," I said, pointing to his magnified eye. "You do look very sleuth-y, though." I surveyed the deep valley. "This is an impossible task. I think we should try a reveal spell."

"I thought you preferred to avoid magic as much as possible."

"You know I do, but we're sort of on the clock here," I said.

"I can do it without you," Neville said. "I'm a wizard in my own right, remember?"

Gratitude curved my lips. "Thanks, Neville."

He trudged through the marsh until he found a bit of solid ground and tucked away his magnifying glass. I kept my gaze on the marshy area as he conducted the spell as though in front of an orchestra. The air rippled around us and I scanned the area for signs of anything supernatural.

"It looks normal," I said. If the demon had been hiding here, it wasn't anymore.

"We should try the marsh nearest to the portal. It's possible the demon was drawn there because of the concentration of energy."

"Good thinking."

We got back in the car and I wished I'd brought mats for the floor. All this mud was going to be a pain to clean.

The next marsh was much smaller than the one near the gorge. Neville pointed to a patch of earth.

"Our demon's been here."

"Can you tell how long ago?" I asked.

Neville crouched near the evidence and studied the area. "No. I think you're right. It rather is like searching for a libido at a werewolf convention."

I laughed. "That's a good one, Neville."

"Under normal circumstances, I'd suggest we try a locator spell," he said.

"How? We don't have anything to use." No fibers or hair. "Wait, what about blood?"

Neville snapped his fingers. "Yes, the blood of its victims," he said. "Excellent idea. Shall we use yours?"

I recoiled. "We can't. My blood is too powerful. It should belong to a human."

"Verity has collected samples, hasn't she?"

"She has. I think Dr. Barton sent her a sample of Henrietta Egerrton's blood. That might work." I hesitated. "Do you think it'll matter if the blood is from someone with a secondary infection or do we need a Patient Zero?"

"I think we need to try whatever we have access to," Neville said. "If it's only a secondary sample, then so be it."

We retreated to the car and swung by Verity's office for a blood sample before riding back to my house. We headed straight to the backyard without going through the house. I didn't need interference from the evil peanut gallery. Princess Buttercup came over to investigate and I let her sniff the vial before throwing a ball for her to fetch.

"I suppose your barn renovation is taking longer than you'd like," Neville said.

"Nothing will happen until John gets better," I said. Thankfully, his symptoms were still minor—a sign of a secondary infection—but I'd worry about him wielding any tools with a fuzzy head. He was likely to lose a finger. At least he'd been spared.

Neville set to work creating the protective circle with rune rocks and I prepared the center. I knew magic use would be inevitable with this job, which was one of the main reasons I never wanted to serve the FBM. More magic means more fury powers and I already had more of those than I wanted. I couldn't begin to guess what would come after wings and immortality. A beak? Talons? I shuddered imagining my future self.

"Are you cold, Agent Fury?" Neville asked.

I hugged myself. "A quick chill. It's gone now." I had to focus on finding this demon. On success. It didn't matter what the personal cost was. People were dying. Supernaturals were sick. I couldn't worry about my own agenda.

"I need to grab a few herbs from inside," I said. "I'll be right back." Clouds were gathering and I sensed moisture in the air.

Princess Buttercup came to sniff Neville and he stiffened. "Her slobber is acidic, isn't it?"

"Sort of," I said. "More like hot springs."

"Sulphuric hot springs," Neville corrected me.

"That's just gas," I called over my shoulder. I hurried into the house and slipped into the pantry without being seen. I hoped to avoid an interrogation by members of my family. Knowing my mother, she'd want to come out and critique my technique.

I collected the herbs I needed and tiptoed out of the pantry. Alice swooped in front of me, nearly causing me to drop the herbs.

"Alice," I hissed. "Don't sneak up on me like that."

"I'm so sorry," Alice said. "I wanted to tell you that I believe I spotted your demon next door earlier."

"Next door? In Mrs. Paulson's yard?"

"That's right. It looked like a large beetle and seemed to take a shine to her vegetable garden."

I hovered in the hallway. Mrs. Paulson was one hundred percent human and elderly. If that demon managed to get its mandibles into her, she was as good as dead.

"Thanks for letting me know, Alice. Do me a favor, if you see it again, will you find me wherever I am?" Alice had the ability to leave her old stomping grounds, she just opted not to most of the time.

"If you think it's that important."

"I do."

"You do what?" My grandmother's voice was like icy fingers down my back.

I spun around. "Nothing. I'm talking to Alice."

Her eyes narrowed. "Where are you going with those herbs?"

"I'm working," I said.

"Why don't you let me help you?" she asked.

I gestured to her robe and bunny slippers. "That's okay. I can see you're busy." I rushed outside before anyone else intercepted me and returned to my place in the circle.

"Ready?" Neville asked.

"Eden, sit up straight," my father's voice boomed. "You're slouching like your body doesn't have a spine."

I opened my eyes and drew a deep breath. "I'm in the middle of a spell, Dad."

"Well, you need better posture or it won't work," he said.

"I don't think the magic is concerned with my posture," I shot back.

"Well, our tree pose worked wonders for the last spell," Neville said. "That's technically a posture."

I glared at him. "Whose side are you on?"

My father folded his arms and observed us. "So what's the spell for?"

"Dad," I said impatiently. "Do you mind? I'm trying to work."

"What? A father can't watch his daughter? What are you so ashamed of? I'm sure you'll manage the spell."

My fists tightened. "I'm not ashamed of anything. I just need to concentrate and that's hard to do when your father is standing over you."

"Hold on." My father walked over and adjusted my top. "Your bra strap was showing."

I groaned. "Dad! Who cares?"

"This isn't a nightclub," my father said. "You're in my yard."

"Technically, I'm in Mom's yard and you're trespassing," I said.

His expression hardened. "You did *not* just go there."

Neville seemed to sense a storm brewing. Literally. Dark clouds clustered above us and thunder rolled in the distance.

"I need to get through this spell without an audience, please," I said. Maybe politeness would work. It didn't always, but one could live in hope.

"Fine," my father snapped. "Sally's making more cheese dip for the festival. I'll go and watch her work since she doesn't have a complex."

I wanted to argue and explain that my complex came from having overbearing parents who constantly berated me for not excelling in evil deeds, but I knew the locator spell was more important than my warped childhood.

"We should hurry," Neville said. "I'm not sure this storm will wait."

I lit the candles and the breeze immediately blew them out. A fat raindrop landed on my hand. "Let me try one more time." I relit the candles and took my place in the circle with Neville. I pulled the vial from my bag and opened the first lid.

As the blood dripped from the vial into the pile of herbs, I heard a sharp intake of breath. I glanced up to see Mrs. Paulson inside the gate. She clutched a basket of muffins to her chest.

"Uh oh," Neville breathed.

"That's an understatement," I said. I forced a smile and waved with my non-vial of blood-holding hand. "Hello, Mrs. Paulson. I think it's about to storm. You should probably head inside."

"Is that blood, Eden?" she asked.

I held up the vial. "This? No, of course not. What makes you think that?"

"Because it looks like blood."

"This is cranberry juice," I said.

"Why are you pouring cranberry juice on a pile of plants?" Mrs. Paulson asked.

"It's a special treatment for the garden," I explained. "Organic pesticide. We're still having trouble with the lemon trees."

"Oh, let me know if it works. I'm still having an issue in my vegetable garden. Your aunt's remedy didn't work."

I popped the lid back on the vial and set it on the ground beside me. "Is there something I can help you with?"

"I came to apologize for the other day," she said. "Bringing the chief over and making such a fuss. It was silly of me."

I jumped to my feet and walked over to the gate to prevent her from getting too close to the circle. There was no way the vial of blood would pass for cranberry juice up close.

"Don't worry about it," I said. "We all make mistakes. Next time, if you would just talk to us before you get the police involved, we would really appreciate it. Communication is so important between neighbors."

"You're so much more pleasant than the others," Mrs. Paulson said. "Well, not Thora. She's all right, too. Knows her way around a garden. I have to respect that."

"My family has a lot of talents, Mrs. Paulson." I only wished they used them to help instead of hurt.

"I like the lady doctor, too," she said. "I don't see her often, though."

"Verity," I said. "My sister-in-law." Verity would spit fire if she heard the phrase 'lady doctor,' not that I blamed her. It was hard to rile up a druid, but Verity's temper spiked when it came to sexism in the medical field.

"The muffins are for you," Mrs. Paulson said. She peered over my shoulder at Neville. "He seems to want your attention."

I twisted to see Neville pointing at the threatening sky and then the circle.

"That's our gardener," I said. "He said we need to get this new pesticide ready before the storm or it'll ruin it."

"I won't keep you then." She thrust the basket into my chest. "They are two kinds. Banana nut and cinnamon."

"Thank you so much. I appreciate the gesture."

"Agent Fury," Neville called.

Mrs. Paulson frowned. "Your gardener calls you Agent Fury?"

"He's very formal." I craned my neck. "Be right there!"

Mrs. Paulson backed away toward the gate, one wary eye pinned on us. Only when she disappeared from view did Neville and I perform the spell. We watched the center of the circle eagerly as the spell revealed—nothing. No location. Nothing at all.

"We need blood from a primary sample," I said. Something we didn't have.

"Right now, we need to seek cover, Agent Fury."

The heavens opened and rain pummeled our circle, dousing the flames and washing away the blood.

"Mother Nature seems angry with us," I said.

"She's not the only one." Neville pointed to the back door, where my mother stood with her hands cemented to her hips.

"Is that my good copper bowl in the rain?" she yelled.

"Sweet Hecate." I scooped up the bowl. "Coming in now!"

"Tell her I'm going back to the office to work on the potion," Neville said. "That'll cheer her up."

I gave him a thumbs up and ran into the house, clutching the bowl under my shirt.

CHAPTER SIXTEEN

CORINNE and I sat at a table in Magic Beans and scrutinized a map of the town. I'd marked all the places we'd discovered the borer demon had been, trying to figure out where it might turn up next. It was pretty much whack-a-demon.

"It likes marshes, but also populated areas," I said.

"Maybe it's an extroverted introvert," Corinne said. "It likes a bit of social interaction but then needs to recharge by itself."

I peered at her. "It's not making lunch plans with an old friend. It's feeding." I tapped the map. "I think it might feed and then go back to the marshes for a post-meal nap."

"So it started with leafy greens and then moved on to flesh and blood?" Corinne appeared disgusted by the idea.

"I think so. It's like a kid who always had to eat healthy suddenly being let loose in a food court."

Corinne shuddered. "I know I've given you a hard time, but I don't know how you do this job, Eden."

"I'm no expert," I said. "Drug trafficking, yes. Demon invasion? Not so much."

"One borer demon hardly qualifies as an invasion."

"It does when it wreaks this much havoc," I said. "Can you imagine what a swarm of them would be capable of? That's why keeping an eye on the portal is so important."

Her expression clouded over. "Because even dormant volcanoes can surprise us every century or so."

My phone buzzed on the table and I glimpsed Clara's picture. "Hey," I said. "I'm in Magic Beans with Corinne."

"Corinne LeRoux?" Clara's shock was evident.

"She's helping me with the case."

"That's why I'm calling," Clara said. "You might want to come down to the promenade."

"Why? What's going on?"

"I saw it," she said in a loud whisper.

"The borer demon?"

"Yes, it's…not as small as I expected."

Great balls of a minotaur. "Where on the promenade?"

"Near Pecorino Place. It shot through some bushes. I'll wait here and show you."

"I'll be right there." I instinctively reached for the hammer in a bag at my feet.

Corrine gave me a curious look. "The demon?"

"Yes."

She grabbed her purse. "I'm coming with you."

"Are you sure? I might need to…kill it," I said. "It could be messy and unpleasant."

She eyed me. "Which part are you uncomfortable with? The messy part or the killing part?"

"Both," I said. "The demon didn't come here on purpose to hurt anyone."

"But it's here now," Corinne said, "and it's hurting people. We have to stop it."

I didn't argue. I knew she felt a sense of responsibility and I wasn't about to deprive her of the chance to make it right.

We left the shop and she locked the door behind us. "I'll

drive. My car's right there." She pointed to a Honda Civic down the block.

"Mine's closer."

"I've seen you drive, Eden Fury," she said. "I'm not playing a role in any more chaos in this town."

"Fair enough." I followed her to the Honda and climbed into the passenger seat. The car was surprisingly grubby with empty wrappers and napkins strewn across the floor and backseat.

"Sorry about the mess," she said. "I let my mom borrow my car this week and haven't had a chance to clean it yet." She started the car and pulled onto the road.

"Why would you clean your mom's mess?" I asked. And why was Rosalie so disrespectful of her daughter's property?

"She's not going to do it," Corinne said matter-of-factly. "So it has to be me."

"Then don't let her borrow your car," I said.

Corinne tossed me a knowing look. "Because it's that easy to say no to family, right?"

I slumped in the seat. "Look, I know it's tough when it's your mom, but she knows magic. Can't she just do a tidying spell?"

Corinne turned onto Roquefort Road. "That's not our kind of magic."

I cut her a quick glance. "What do you mean?"

"I mean I don't know a cleanup spell and I doubt my mother does either. Our coven's magic is more elemental."

"I didn't know that."

"I bet there's a lot we don't know about each other."

I sneezed in triplicate. "Happen to have any clean tissues in this mess?"

She angled her head toward me. "Under your seat there should be a box."

I reached under and, sure enough, there was a rectangular

tissue box. I blew my nose. "I hope Neville finishes that potion today so I can start distributing it."

"Any idea how you'll get the humans to take it?"

"Verity said she'll take care of it. I'll handle the supernaturals."

"Not by yourself," Corinne said. "Whatever you need, I'm available."

"Thanks."

Corinne parallel parked the car between two jeeps with the deft skill of a city girl.

"Two points to Hufflepuff," I said, motioning to the park job.

Corinne scrunched her nose. "Do I look like a Hufflepuff to you?"

"I don't know. What does a Hufflepuff look like?"

"I'm clearly a Gryffindor," she said.

"I guess that makes me a Slytherin," I said. Big surprise.

We vacated the car and hurried to where Clara waited on the promenade. She was texting on her phone when we arrived.

"I'm supposed to be down here covering the new flower beds that the town put in," Clara said with a roll of her eyes.

"Front page news there," Corinne said.

"Cawdrey's been sick so you'd think my assignments would improve," Clara said.

"Let me guess," I said. "Cal is sitting on all the good stories until his star reporter is better?"

"Something like that." Clara pointed to the bushes. "There's the trail."

It looked as though something had cut a hole straight through the bushes. "It made a tunnel."

"I didn't think it would be smart to chase it," Clara said.

"No, not with your human blood," I said. "Too risky."

"Do you want me to wait here in case it circles back?" Clara asked.

I shook my head. "No, I don't want to endanger you. Corinne and I will follow the trail and see where it leads. You just stay clear of the area."

"I'll head back to the office and write up the scintillating story of the flower beds," Clara said.

"Thanks for letting me know. You've been a huge help." I shifted my focus to Corinne. "Are you ready?"

"You've got the hammer, right?" Corinne asked.

I removed it from the bag. "The only kind of accessory I'm into these days, much to my mother's chagrin."

"I bet I can find you a pair of earrings to match the handle," Corinne joked.

Clara made herself scarce as Corinne and I ventured into the bushes.

"Here, scary magic beetle. Here, boy," I called. I pushed aside the wall of greenery and scoured the area for the demon's trail.

Corinne arched an eyebrow. "Why not just throw a tennis ball and see if the demon chases it?"

I sneezed. "My symptoms are flaring up. I wonder if that means the demon's close by."

"Or could be that you're smack in the middle of nature."

"It's not allergies," I said. My throat begat to tickle. "Okay, maybe it is. Gods, I hate this."

"You have access to powerful magic," Corinne said. "Can't you use a locator spell or a tracking spell?"

"I've tried and failed," I said. "This thing moves fast and often. The demon's already gone by the time you get there." I halted. "Like right now." I let loose an agitated groan. "I think we lost it."

Corinne looked at me askance. "I get that it's your job, but everyone has a vested interest in stopping this demon. You should ask for help."

"I've had help," I said.

Corinne gestured to the bushes around us. "Help for this. You know good trackers. Use them."

She was right. There were plenty of others willing to pitch in.

"Oh, and just so you know, I asked out the chief," Corinne said.

My heart stuttered. "And?"

Corinne smiled. "I believe his exact words were—'sure, why not?'"

"He seems like a great guy. Good luck with him," I said, because I had no idea what else to say. I pulled out my phone and tapped the screen, swallowing a frustrated cry in the process.

"Julie," I said, pushing down the lump in my throat. "I need the pack's help."

"Okay, listen up," I said, injecting as much authority into my voice as I could muster. "I need your tracking skills because I've been chasing ghosts and I can't afford any more casualties."

I had a small team of werewolves assembled in front of me—Julie, Meg, Hugh, and his sister, Paisley. We stood by the river not far from the vortex.

"And you want us to track a beetle, General?" Hugh asked.

I ignored his jab. "Not just any beetle," I said. "It's a borer demon. From what I can tell, it's been growing larger with every feed."

"What about its scent?" Meg asked. She frowned. "Does a beetle have a scent?"

"I have a few specimens that should help," I said. I

unzipped the backpack with leaves from the marsh as well as fragments of the bush the demon tunneled through at the promenade. "Sniff to your heart's content."

"You have siphoning powers," Hugh said. "Why not leech off one of us and become a wolf yourself?"

I hesitated. "I try to limit the magic I use."

"It drains her energy," Julie added. "If she turns into a werewolf and finds the demon, she might not have the strength to fight it."

I sent her a silent thank you. My cousin understood that the more powers I used, the more the gods gave me. Anytime I could find a way of achieving the same result without my supernatural abilities, that would be my choice every single time.

"Plus wolf paws make it hard to hold a mystical hammer," I said.

"And we can see this demon, right?" Meg asked.

"Any supernaturals can," I said. "It's only invisible to humans."

"This is a serious matter. A direct bite can result in death for humans."

"Then we need to kill it," Hugh added. "Squash this demon like the bug it truly is."

"That's what the hammer's for," I said.

"Grind it into the ground," Paisley continued. "Turn that beetle body into dust."

I'd forgotten how violent werewolves could be.

"What do we do if one of us finds the demon then?" Julie asked. "We won't have the hammer."

"Call me immediately," I said. "Don't try to attack it. If you try to kill it by any other method, it won't work. It's like a cockroach that way."

Julie gave her daughter a pointed look. "See? This is when a phone would come in handy."

"Who doesn't have a phone?" Hugh asked.

"Miss Retro Hipster over here," Julie said.

Meg rolled her eyes. "I'll send smoke signals."

Her mother put a hand on her hip. "Oh, so a phone is the devil, but smoking is okay?"

"Smoke *signals*, Mom." Meg smacked her head.

"Maybe we should track together so you don't end up alone in a ditch," Julie said. "Your father would never forgive me."

"If I end up alone in a ditch—I'm a werewolf—I'll *simply climb out*," Meg said.

Hugh snickered. "You ladies don't need to worry. If anyone can track the borer demon, it's me."

"You can't even track a local bride," Julie said. "That's why you had to import one."

Hugh's growl was low but audible. "And the sooner we find this pest, the sooner I get to my honeymoon night, so let's get on with it."

"How do you all plan to carry your phones in wolf form?" I asked. "Is there some kind of kangaroo pouch for your personal items?"

Hugh whipped up his shirt to show me a strap underneath where his phone was safely nestled against his skin. "It's designed by a werewolf to stay attached even after shifting."

"I wish I'd invented it," Paisley said. "I'd be rich."

"Mine's monogrammed," Hugh said.

Of course it was.

"What will you do?" Paisley asked me.

"I'm going to work with Neville on distributing the potion," I said. "But I'll be there in a pinch if you call." I'd cloak myself and use my wings if I had to.

"At my signal," Hugh began, but the women had already shifted. "Hey!"

I stifled a laugh. "You were saying, alpha?"

He glowered at me before shifting and running off into the woods.

I trudged to my car and drove to the office where Neville was loading the potion bottles into boxes.

"You're sure these will do the trick?" I asked.

"Take one and find out." He handed me a small bottle.

I downed the potion. "Minty."

"I thought it would help if I masked the taste."

"Get the first delivery to the nursing home. I'll let Verity know in case she wants to oversee it."

"Where will you go?" Neville asked.

"I'll handle the young crowd and we'll work our way to the less vulnerable." Like my mother.

"Sounds like a plan, Agent Fury."

"Thank you for your work on this, Neville. You're truly saving lives."

I enlisted Corinne's help in distributing as many of the potion bottles as possible. She called her grandmother, too, who called Husbourne and Aggie Grace. It was all hands on deck and I appreciated it.

I checked my phone throughout the day, but there was no word from the wolves. To say I was disappointed was an understatement.

Finally, Julie's name flashed on my screen and I scrambled to answer the phone, nearly dropping it on the kitchen floor in the process.

"Julie, where are you?"

"Calm down, Eden. I don't have it. I'm sorry."

"Did you see any sign of it?"

"Lots of signs of it, but it's smart and fast," Julie said. "We're calling it a day."

"All of you?" I figured at least Hugh would be stubborn.

"Hugh's mail-order bride kept texting him to come home,

so he finally gave in," Julie said. "She wants his opinion on seating arrangements for the wedding."

"He's quite the alpha," I said. "Thank you for your help."

"We can try again tomorrow," Julie said. "The dark's no good. It's black and doesn't have much of a scent. Kind of puts our tracking skills to the test."

"I understand. I'll talk to you tomorrow." I hung up the phone and sighed.

"No luck, huh?" Aunt Thora asked.

"Not yet." I forced a smile. "We'll get it, Aunt Thora."

"Darn straight. No quitters in this house." She paused. "Unless you count your mother's divorce. I suppose that's technically quitting a marriage."

"You're supposed to be the nice one," I said accusingly.

Grandma shuffled into the kitchen. "Ha! Thora? That's only because you didn't know her when she was younger. She put the wicked in...wicked."

"That's enough, Esther," Aunt Thora said. "Those days are long behind me and you know it."

"If anyone needs me, I'll be hiding in the barn in shameful defeat." I expected a snappy retort, but they observed me in silence. I threw out my arms. "What? No criticism? This is the part where you kick me when I'm down."

Grandma opened her mouth, but Aunt Thora's hand clamped over it before she could speak. "Not today, Eden. Not today."

CHAPTER SEVENTEEN

I stood in the empty barn in quiet contemplation. It wasn't my home yet, but that didn't mean I couldn't use it. According to Verity, John had taken the potion and should recover soon, but he was still at risk until the demon was caught. We all were.

Anton's silhouette appeared in the oversized doorway. "Brooding, table for one?"

"Hey, big brother."

"You look like you have the weight of the world on your shoulders."

I shrugged. "Just the town."

"I hate to add to your malaise, but Verity asked me to tell you there's been a death at the nursing home."

My heart plummeted. "Not Henrietta, I hope."

"Derek Mahon," he replied. "Ninety. He came down with flu-like symptoms twenty-four hours ago. He got the potion, but it was too late to save him."

I resisted the urge to burst into tears. Instead, I dropped onto an overturned crate. "I should be good at this. Why am I so terrible?"

"He was ninety, Eden," Anton said, slightly exasperated. "He lived a long life for a human."

"But he died from supernatural causes," I said. "That's my only job in this town, to protect people from Otherworld influences and I'm failing miserably."

He knocked on one of the slabs of wood, still waiting to find its place in the barn. "You've really been thrown into the deep end of this job, haven't you?"

I laughed bitterly. "And here I thought Paul sat around all day, eating peanuts out of a jar and waiting for excitement to come along." I felt so foolish. I'd actually asked the FBI psychiatrist if he'd died from boredom.

"I think he did," Anton said. "Well, I don't know about the peanuts, but I never got the impression that he was busy hunting demons. You seem to have taken this job to a whole new level. Typical Eden."

I hugged my knees to my chest. "No, you're right. Neville seems like a horse that's finally been let out of the barn. He's getting to use more of his skills and he loves it."

"Don't forget Neville's also been doing this longer than you," Anton said. "Not to mention the fact that he hasn't spent years trying to hide his true nature."

I met my brother's sympathetic gaze. "I'm still hiding it, Anton. Every supernatural in this town has to do the same. Unless we all move to Otherworld, that's our lot in life."

"We have plenty of opportunities to be our authentic ourselves here, though," he said. "There's strength in numbers."

"Speaking of our authentic selves, how's your side hustle?" I asked. Although Anton's day job was in creative advertising, he wasn't completely out of the vengeance demon game.

He shoved his hands in his pockets. "I told you I've scaled back. And I keep my shenanigans out of this territory."

"What about Olivia and Ryan?" I asked. "How are you going to keep them out of the axis of evil?"

"Verity is their mother," he said. "She's a strong druid and an even stronger woman. She doesn't want them to succumb to the dark side any more than you do."

I gave a crisp nod. He was right. Verity possessed a quiet strength that was often overlooked in our house. We were too accustomed to noise and aggression.

"Is that what attracted you to her?" I asked.

"No, that was the tight sweater she was wearing the day we met."

I groaned. "Figures."

He kicked the crate out from under me and I fell to the floor. "But it didn't take me long after that to figure out she was the one for me. I had to work hard for it, though. She wasn't interested."

"Because she could tell you were a damp squib."

"Nothing damp about my squib until both parties have been satisfied."

I groaned louder.

He grinned. "That's not quite the right sound, but you're close."

I shot to my feet. "Gross, Anton."

"Anyway, my point is that Verity didn't want anything to do with me because of our family's reputation. I had to prove that I was willing to change. I had to earn her."

"Men don't change," I said. "That's a myth."

"Do you think I shifted away from vengeance because I suddenly grew a conscience?" he asked. "That was Verity's influence."

"She nagged the evil out of you?" Now there was a trick.

"Have you ever heard her nag? No. She showed me how to live a better life by example. How to be a better supernatural in this world." He picked up a two by four and swung it like a baseball bat. "Do you think I wanted to end up like Mom and Dad?"

"Nobody wants that," I said quietly.

"Dad loves being a vengeance demon," Anton said. "It's all he knows and he'll never change. He and Mom were too volatile together."

"There was no balance," I said. "Too much yin and no yang."

"Verity and I have softened each other's edges," Anton said. "She's learned to accept the complexity of my nature, that she can love someone capable of terrible things."

"Capable is the salient word in that sentence," I said.

"The truth is we're all capable of terrible things, Eden, even your cowboy."

I perked up. "My cowboy?"

"Chief Fox. He walks around with a gun. He's trained to kill."

"He would never…"

"He would if he had to," Anton interjected. "That's the job. To deal the death blow is a terrible thing, regardless of the reason. The older my children get, the more I see it."

I stared at my big brother in awe. I'd never heard him sound so…mature.

"Maybe you and the chief aren't as impossible as you think," Anton continued. "You'd soften each other's edges the way Verity and I have."

"It's different," I said. "Verity is a druid. Chief Fox is pure human. The guy's from Iowa, for gods' sake. He's shocked by the scandalous variety of pizza here."

Anton chuckled. "Give the guy some credit. He might just enjoy a little sriracha on his corn on the cob."

"He might get some, but it won't be from me." I couldn't bear to tell him about Corinne, not when I was already feeling so low.

I waved my hands. "Okay, that's enough pep talk from you. I think I like it better when we bicker."

"That's your comfort level," Anton said. "But we're working on it, right? I don't want us to be like Mom and Grandma."

I smiled. "That's only because you don't have resurrection powers."

"It does put me at a distinct disadvantage," he said.

"Don't worry," I said. "Killing has never been my jam. Just ask the borer demon."

"Nobody really cares whether you kill it, Eden. Just that it stops terrorizing the town."

I nodded gravely. "That's all I want, too."

"Why don't we drop in on Dad and Sally?" Anton asked. "We never go over together. It might freak him out. Come on, it'll be fun."

"I know what you're doing," I said.

Anton cast me a sidelong glance. "Good. Let me know because I don't have a clue."

"You're not letting me mope. You figure if I keep busy, I won't succumb to my feelings of failure."

He straightened and smiled. "I was going with misery loves company, but yours makes me sound pretty clever. I like it."

Together, we crossed the yard until we entered my father's house via the kitchen.

"Hey, Dad..." I stopped abruptly when I spotted Michael Bannon in the living room.

"Eden, Anton, you've met Mr. Bannon, haven't you?" Sally asked. "He moved into Dudley's old house recently."

"Yes," I said carefully.

Anton frowned. "This is the guy who's been raging on our doorstep?"

"Raging?" my father asked. "At my children?"

Michael stood. "I'm afraid so."

"It's okay, Dad," I said. Michael did *not* want to get on the wrong side of a vengeance demon.

"I'm sorry we got off on the wrong foot, Eden," Michael said. "The move has been emotional for me and I've not been acting like myself."

I knew this, of course, but I had to feign ignorance. "I'm sorry to hear that, but I appreciate the apology."

"Michael golfs," my father said. "Isn't that terrific news?"

"For whom?" Sally asked.

"For me," my father said. "Who else? It'll be nice to have a neighbor to take to the country club."

"What about Husbourne?" I asked.

My father scrunched his nose. "He always insists on wearing those zany outfits. It's embarrassing."

"Linen suits are embarrassing?" I asked.

"In all those cotton candy colors they are," my father said.

"I was just telling Michael about the cheese festival," Sally said. "It's such a great opportunity to see the town at its best."

"Plus, cheese," I said. "You can't go wrong there."

Michael gave me an unapologetic look. "Actually, my doctor put cheese on the restricted list. Heart attack city for me."

The four of us gasped in horror.

"No cheese?" my father said. "What kind of monster hands down a decree like that?"

"It's practically a death sentence," Sally added.

"No, eating the cheese would be a death sentence," Michael said.

"Well, you should come anyway," I said. "There are lots of other non-cheese stalls, plus performances and beer."

"Everybody in town is there," Sally said. "It'll be a good chance to meet people."

Michael smiled. "You mean people I haven't already offended."

"My family has forgotten by now," I said. "Their memories are short."

My father slapped his thigh. "Nice try, Eden! Your mother has the memory of the Bible."

"The Bible?" I shot back. "Are you sure that's the reference you want to be making?"

"The Bible remembers everything," my father said. "Who begat who. All the betrayals. It's basically a tell-all."

"Who begat whom," Sally corrected him.

"I've been wanting to apologize to your family," Michael said. "I just haven't worked up the nerve. I'm mortified."

"They don't need an apology," my father said. "Trust me, they'll be offending you far more than you could ever offend them."

A thought occurred to me. "Have you met Mrs. Paulson yet?"

"Your neighbor on the other side?" Michael asked.

"Yes, she's a widow," Sally said. "Lives on her own."

"I owe her an apology, too," Michael said sheepishly. "I interrogated her about my car. To her credit, though, she handled it like a champ."

"How so?" I asked.

"She hit me with her giant tote bag and told me to get off her property or she'd call the police." He chuckled. "She's a tough one."

"She likes donuts," I said. "Boston cream from Holes."

Michael broke into a smile. "Thanks for the tip."

"Let me know when you're ready to apologize to my family and I can make sure I'm there," I said. "Stand next to you in the event of retaliation." A sneeze threatened to overtake me and I shoved my elbow in front of my face to protect everyone from the fallout.

"Eden, your posture is worse than a Bavarian pretzel," my father said.

"First, pretzels don't have posture," I said. "Second, I had to sneeze. Of course I hunched over."

Michael looked me over. "Your father's right. My great-aunt Ethel had terrible posture and ended up with osteoporosis. She couldn't stand straight if she wanted to. She said it made sex really uncomfortable." He wagged a finger at me. "Something to think about."

I grimaced. "You want me to think about your great-aunt's awkward sex life? I thought you were trying not to offend me."

"He's right, though," my father said. "No man is going to be interested in a hunchback."

"I'm not trying to attract a man," I said.

"Not in that outfit," Sally said.

"Is nowhere safe around here to be myself?"

"You can be yourself," my father said, "just be a prettier version."

I closed my eyes for a brief moment and collected myself.

Anton slung an arm across my shoulders. "I think we've soaked up all the fun we can here tonight. Sally, good luck with your cheese dip at the festival tomorrow. Michael, it was nice meeting you." He steered me out of the living room and toward the kitchen door. "I have to say, you have some thick skin, sister."

I smiled up at him as we left the house. "A lifetime of training, Anton. If the next supernatural event involves an insult demon, I'm all set."

CHAPTER EIGHTEEN

THE DAY of the annual cheese festival was bright and cheerful. Blue skies above and puffy white clouds full of promise.

"Oh, how I still look forward to the festival each year," Alice said, hovering next to me at the attic window. "All that delicious cheese. I still remember how it tastes." She closed her eyes and smiled. "I had my first kiss at the festival."

"Really? That wasn't scandalous?"

"Well, I didn't tell anyone," Alice said. "It was my special secret." She clasped her hands in front of her. "Maybe you'll meet someone today."

I laughed. "At the cheese festival? Kind of difficult when I'm not going."

"You should go," Alice said. "There might be a handsome supernatural visiting from out of town. The event attracts people from far and wide."

"Honestly, Alice, I'm not looking to meet anyone. My life is busy enough."

"Because you're infatuated with Chief Fox," Alice said.

"Infatuated is a bit strong," I said. "Let's just say I have a preference for him."

"That you can't act on." Alice clucked her tongue. "Such a waste of hormones."

"I don't think you can really waste hormones, Alice, but I appreciate the thought." I got dressed and brushed my hair before venturing downstairs. Today was a new day and I was determined to make it count.

"Good morning, all," I said, as I entered the kitchen. The aroma of fresh bread wafted over to me. "Aunt Thora, I smell your handiwork."

"It'll be protein the rest of the day for Verity and the children," she replied. "I thought it would be nice to get their carbs in now."

"I'm happy to slather butter on my bread," I said. I took a seat next to Anton at the table.

Aunt Thora pushed the butter dish closer to me. "Have at it."

"Are you excited for the festival, Olivia?" I asked. "Grandma Sally is making a special cheese dip that you might like to try. And there'll be lots of stalls…"

"I don't like this," my mother said warily.

I glanced up at her. "Like what?"

My mother zigzagged a finger in front of me. "This whole Friend of FromageFest attitude from you."

"Why dampen the children's enthusiasm?" I asked. "I'm seeing it through new eyes."

Olivia gaped at me. "You have *new* eyes, Aunt Eden?" She turned toward her Verity. "Mommy, can I have new eyes? These are still too leaky from my cold."

"They look back to normal to me," Verity said.

My niece appeared thoughtful. "I don't think a magic bug bit me. I think it was Ryan."

"Your brother did not bite you," Anton said.

Grandma leaned forward with her elbows on the table. "Tell me more, Olivia. Maybe your brother is finally showing some personality."

"And by personality, you mean demonic traits," I said.

"Potato, tomato," Grandma replied.

Olivia tickled her brother's chin. "Did you bite me, Ryan? I don't think so, did you?" she asked in a baby voice. "Because I would smite you before you even started preschool. Yes, I would."

Anton and I exchanged glances. He and I weren't exactly best friends growing up, but we never killed each other the way the witch trio did.

"Um, Olivia, that's not a very nice thing to say to your brother," Verity said.

"Are you kidding?" my mother asked. "Olivia is showing him who's boss. Nothing wrong with a little feminism."

"That's not feminism," I said. "That's plain scary."

My mother shook her head in dismay. "The goal post is always being moved by you, isn't it?"

"Let's eat so we can get to the festival," Grandma said.

My hand froze before the bread made it to my mouth. "You're not going to the festival, remember?"

"I have to go this year," Grandma said. "I want to see if Giorgio Kincaid is there."

I gave her a curious look. "Why?"

"Because his wife died last week," Grandma said.

"Oh, that's nice of you," I said. And very uncharacteristic. "You want to make sure he's getting out of the house?"

"No, I want to make sure that I get to him before the other widows," Grandma said. "It isn't every day we add another eligible bachelor to our ranks in this town."

"Isn't he human?" Verity asked.

Grandma shrugged. "I won't hold that against him."

"Why not?" I asked. "You hold it against Chief Fox."

"That's different," Grandma said. "He's the chief of police and you're an FBM agent. You're also both young enough to get married and have children. You can't do that with a human."

"She can," Verity said. "It's physically possible."

"Fine, I misspoke," Grandma said. "You *shouldn't* do that with a human."

"And you *shouldn't* go to the festival," I said. "Because if you end up there, that means I'll end up there to put out whatever literal fires you start."

"If someone sees you, they'll report you," Aunt Thora said.

"So let them report me," Grandma said. "I'll hex them so badly, they'll never want to touch another slice of cheese for the rest of their lives."

"At least glamour yourself," I said.

"And don't come within five feet of us," Verity warned. "It's bad enough that Anton can't join us."

Anton drummed his fingers on the table. "I've decided to come this year."

Olivia cheered. "Will you really, Daddy?"

Anton gave her a firm nod. "This should be a family outing and I'm part of your family."

I bit my lip. "Please use common sense. I need to focus on this demon. I don't have time to deal with a crisis started by my own family."

"We'll be on our best behavior," Grandma said.

I stared at her. "That's not good enough and you know it."

"Just grab your hammer, Thor, and quit making a fuss," Grandma said. "You have other priorities today. There's still a borer demon on the loose, remember?"

Kind of hard to forget. "Have fun. Bring home lots of samples."

"Don't worry, Eden," mother said. "I'm staying home, too, until tonight that is. The bars will be packed later." She perked up. "We usually get our share of sailors at this event."

"You've already had your share of sailors," Grandma snapped.

I retreated to the attic before the conversation escalated. I refused to bury a body today unless it was in the shape of a beetle.

I stretched out on my mattress and studied the map of the demon's travel patterns. There was no rhyme or reason. Then again, we were hunting a supernatural beetle, so why would there be?

Hedwig's Theme from Harry Potter burst from my phone. I tapped the screen. "Hey, Neville. What have you got for me?"

"I hate to tell you this, but there's been a sighting," Neville said.

"Why would you hate to tell me?" I asked, moving to a seated position. "That's great news."

I heard the sound of Neville's deep inhalation through the phone. "The sighting took place near Pimento Plaza."

"Okay, so it's downtown," I replied. "That's no..." The realization slammed into me like a boot in the stomach. "Great balls of fury. It's at the festival."

"I'm sorry, my liege," he said. "I didn't want to be the bearer of bad news."

I closed my eyes and tried to stay calm. A supernatural pest with the power to spread more germs than a sneezing kindergartner with grabby hands was on the prowl at the busiest event of the year.

"I guess that settles it," I said. "I'm heading to Cheese-chella after all."

The entire downtown area was lined with cheese stalls and other offerings. A huge banner hung between lamp posts that read *Make Chipping Cheddar Grate Again*. Some poor soul in a mouse costume danced along the sidewalk, shaking paws with children. I wasn't a fan of mice, so this guy was the stuff of nightmares as far as I was concerned.

I caught sight of Clara and Sassy over by the brie stall and waved. Clara motioned for me to join them. Thankfully, there was no sign of Tanner.

"Hello, ladies," I said. "Drunk on red wine cheese yet?"

"We've already been stuffing ourselves," Clara said. "The raclette on toast is amazing."

"You're allowed to be here?" Sassy eyed me closely.

"I'm a federal agent," I said. "Chief Fox wants me here."

"More like he just wants you," Sassy said. "Not that I'm at all jealous. Not even a little bit."

Clara nudged her. "Not every guy needs to be in love with you. Save some for the rest of us."

"Why on earth are you carrying a backpack?" Sassy asked. "You're not in high school."

"It's to take food home," I lied. No need to reveal the truth about the supernatural weapon in my bag.

"If only you could fit the world's largest wheel of cheese," Clara said, inclining her head toward the sign.

"You caught me red-handed. Who can resist the world's largest wheel of cheese?" I asked. A dubious claim, but the wheel *was* pretty big.

"Me," Sassy said. "I can. Way too much fat."

Hedwig's Theme emanated from my pocket. "Sorry, I got distracted."

"Brie stall," Neville said. "I've been following from a safe distance, but he's quick."

"Hasn't stopped for a bite to eat?" I asked.

"Not that I've seen. You should hurry, though."

I hung up the phone. "I'll catch up with you later. I need to meet Neville."

"Somebody has a crush," Sassy said in a singsong voice.

I frowned at her. "It's called a work colleague. Not every member of the opposite sex is a romantic interest."

Sassy's blond ponytail bobbed up and down. "That's true. I mean, look at the men at *The Buttermilk Bugle*." She wrinkled her nose. "No thanks."

My phone started to sing again. "Nice catching up, but I really need to go." I sprinted toward the brie stall without a second glance.

And there was my target. I watched as the borer demon scampered behind the neighboring camembert stall. Clara was right—the demonic beetle was big now, easily the size of a sofa cushion. There was no time to lose. I opened the backpack and rushed forward, hammer in hand. Humans still wouldn't be able to see the pest, but supernaturals would and they might inadvertently start a stampede if I didn't get to the demon first.

Now.

"Neville," I yelled. "I have eyes on our friend."

The wizard was beside me in a nanosecond. "I'll help you corner it."

He raced around one side of the stall and I took the other route. We found the borer demon sat in a clump of overgrown grass, munching on a wedge of Manchego cheese. It stopped when it spotted us closing in. In larger size, it was actually kind of cute with those big black eyes.

"I don't want to kill it," I said.

"You've got to use the hammer," Neville insisted. "The entire purpose of that weapon is to eradicate the species. It's a pest, Agent Fury. It brings nothing to this world except disease."

Ugh, but still. It was a living creature. What right did I have to act as its judge, jury, and executioner?

"Think of it this way," Neville continued, "if you don't kill it with the hammer, the borer demon will go on to kill more innocent humans. Their infected blood will be on your hands."

I pointed at the adorable demon. "But look," I said. "He's eating cheese now. He's not infecting anyone."

At that precise moment, the demon dropped the cheese and lunged at me, snapping its giant mandibles.

"Great beetle balls," I said and swiped at it with the hammer.

The demon made a strange hissing sound and moved slowly toward me.

"Not so adorable now, is it?" Neville asked.

"Oh, sure. Rub it in." I kept my eyes locked on the demon. One wrong move and I would be wrestling a giant version of a beetle in the middle of the cheese festival.

The demon bolted right and I raced after it, swinging my hammer as I ran. I nearly caught its back end, but missed and whacked the side of the gruyere stall instead.

"Sorry," I called. I knew I looked insane. To anyone without the Sight, I was racing around the festival with a chunky scythe and deliberately destroying the stalls. As horrible as that was, I didn't have time to figure out a solution. The demon was the priority. If too many people were bitten, the epidemic would explode to epic proportions and the demon could become too large to defeat on my own.

The demon flanked left and scooted under another stall before I could reach it.

"Agent Fury, what in the hell are you doing?" Chief Fox stood on the corner, gaping at me.

I glanced at the weird weapon in my hand. "I can explain."

"Is this some kind of retaliation for banning your family?" the chief asked. He crossed the street to talk to me. "Because destruction of property is hardly the type of behavior expected of a federal agent...or you."

"You don't understand." Of course he didn't. How could

he? There was an entire secret world around him that he knew nothing about and I was responsible for keeping it that way.

He crossed his arms over his firm chest. "Enlighten me."

I tried to ignore the way his biceps rippled beneath the thin fabric of his shirt. "One of the stalls was breaking and I brought this special tool to help repair it."

"Which stall?"

"The one with cheese," I replied lamely. A scream erupted from two stalls away. "I need to go, Chief."

"What is it?"

My feet itched to move, but the rest of me wanted to stay and explain everything. Finally, I said, "Do you trust me?"

"With that thing? I don't know." He rubbed his dimpled chin and my body felt like melted cheese.

"Chief, I can't explain, but I ask you to trust me." I didn't wait for a response. I took off in the direction of the scream.

"Here," Neville yelled. He had the borer demon cornered again, this time against a brick wall behind a row of stalls selling fresh vegetables, not as popular as cheese.

The demon was too fast. It skirted Neville and headed back toward the brie stall. Luckily, festival attendees were far too wrapped up in their cheese-related fun to notice a creature so low to the ground as it darted from stall to stall.

Neville and I cornered it again, this time behind the display of the world's largest wheel of cheese, which at least kept us hidden from view. Everyone was busy admiring the wheel from the other side.

"What are you doing back here?" Grandma croaked.

"Stay back," I said in a loud whisper.

She caught sight of the demon beetle. "Oh. This is the guy, huh? Doesn't look like much."

The demon hissed again. It seemed to know it was truly trapped this time. As I held the hammer over my head and prepared to drive it downward, compassion stilled my hand. The borer demon didn't deserve to die. It was only being true to its nature and feeding. Yes, I had an obligation to protect the population of this town from supernatural shenanigans, but this demon wasn't a malevolent force. It wasn't attacking people because it was vicious and cruel. It didn't even ask to come here. The demon had simply been attracted to the coffee beans and inadvertently ended up in Corrine's shop.

I gripped the glowing hammer and swung it—but not at the demon. At the last second, I twisted and connected with the giant wheel of cheese.

"Move!" I yelled.

Neville and Grandma jumped toward me as the display came crashing down on top of the beetle, trapping it within its scooped out center.

I touched Grandma's arm and quickly siphoned her magic. I cut my palm and placed a bloody hand on the chunk of cheese, creating a ward around the wheel. It had to be a blood ward because the demon had already proven it could break through the basic protective ward around the lemon trees. Even if it ate its way through the cheese, there'd be no escape for the borer demon until the wheel was delivered safely to Otherworld.

"The package is secure," Neville said.

"Thanks, I can see that."

Grandma's legs crumpled beneath her. Neville managed to slide an arm around her waist to stop her from falling.

"What did you do that for?" Grandma asked, shooting me a menacing look. "Use your own..." She stopped abruptly before she used the word 'magic.' Too many witnesses had gathered to investigate the commotion.

"I needed a shortcut," I said, panting a little. Thankfully, I didn't need too much magic, so the siphoning didn't wipe me out.

"Yuck. Why is there blood on the largest wheel of cheese?" someone asked.

Mrs. Hughes stepped closer. "You've destroyed the festival's best display," she said, shaking a finger at me. "Your first year back and look what you've done."

"It was an accident," I lied. "I hurt myself." Of course, she couldn't see the borer demon and I couldn't explain its existence.

Mrs. Hughes pulled out her phone. "I'm calling the chief to report this act of aggression."

"Aggression," Grandma said, incensed. She shook off Neville's arm and took a wobbly step forward. "I'll show you an act of aggression, you ungrateful piece of plastic."

Mrs. Hughes's fingers flew to touch her Botoxed face. "How dare you threaten me. You shouldn't even be allowed here. This is exactly why your family was banned in the first place."

A small crowd had assembled and I didn't want to create any more of a spectacle. I'd done enough damage for one day.

I shoved the mystical hammer into my backpack and looped my arm through Grandma's. "Come on. We should go. There's plenty of cheese back at the house."

I had to calm Grandma before she retaliated. As much as I disliked Tanner's mother, I couldn't unleash Grandma on her. Nobody deserved that.

"What about the display?" Neville asked.

"It's too dangerous to leave up," I said quickly. "That thing is clearly a liability. The town could be sued. There was a case just like this in Nebraska and the town had to pay millions. My Uncle Moyer told me all about it."

Excited chatter erupted among the onlookers. I decided to take the opportunity to haul the wheel to safety. I could've lifted it by myself, of course, but I couldn't let the people see my true strength. Like the borer demon, some things were best left invisible to the human eye.

"Neville, wait here while I drum up some helpers." Anton and my father were here somewhere. Probably Uncle Moyer and Tomas, too.

"To do what?" Neville asked.

"Push it back to an upright position, and then we can roll it away."

"To where?" Neville asked.

It was too big to fit in my office. "Davenport Park, near the mound." I'd contact FBM headquarters to dispatch an extraction team immediately.

"Are you sure you don't want my help?" Grandma asked. "I'd be happy to take care of any number of things here." If her eyes could shoot daggers, Mrs. Hughes would be Swiss cheese right now.

"We're good, thanks," I said. "You should go home. One giant mess is more than enough to clean up for one day."

CHAPTER NINETEEN

I woke up the next day feeling back to my normal self, a sure sign that the potion had worked and the borer demon had been safely returned to Otherworld.

I opened the window of the attic and was greeted by the echo of a hammer on a nail. John was back in the barn and hard at work. Thank the gods.

"Good morning, sunshine," Alice said. She swept across the attic. "From the chatter downstairs, it sounds like all's well that end's well."

I turned toward her. "I suppose."

"That statement hardly rings with enthusiasm," Alice said. "You defeated the demon, used your blood, and didn't gain any new fury powers. Isn't that what you consider a success?"

I offered a sad smile. "You're right, Alice. It is a resounding success."

"Then why so glum?"

I crossed the attic and changed into running shorts and a T-shirt. "I'm not glum. I'm fine. It's a beautiful day and everything is as it should be." I slipped on socks and shoes and headed for the steps.

Alice whooshed in front of me. "Bullshit." She gasped at her own language. "Oh, my. Where did that come from?"

I stopped in my tracks. "I'm allowed to feel sad, okay? It's a basic emotion."

"I'm not saying you shouldn't," Alice said. "It seems surprising when you have so much to celebrate. That's all." She scrutinized me. "Unless something happened with the chief."

I lowered my gaze. "Something happened with the chief and then something else happened."

"That's…fairly vague," Alice said. "Care to elaborate?"

I let loose the breath I was holding. "He's moving on."

Alice floated out of my path. "I see. Is this because you rejected his advances?"

"I guess so. Corinne LeRoux asked him out and he said yes."

"A witch." Alice wore a sympathetic expression. "In some ways, that's worse, isn't it?"

"In a lot of ways," I admitted. "I expected him to settle down with a nice human and live a safe life." That was what I wanted for him—happiness and safety.

"Does Corinne realize she's stepping on toes?"

"I gave her my blessing," I said. "She thinks what he thinks —that I'm not really interested."

"What are you going to do about it?" Alice asked.

"The only thing I can do—nothing." I headed downstairs and tried to shake off the feelings of sadness and disappointment. Now that the demon outbreak was over, the emotions that had been waiting in the wings were now flooding my system. I didn't choose to be a fury or an FBM agent. I didn't choose to be part of this maddening family and live in Chipping Cheddar. But I chose to keep Chief Fox at arm's length for his own protection and I had to accept the consequences.

Princess Buttercup met me at the bottom of the steps. She

was wrapped in a silk scarf and had a glittering butterfly clipped to one of her ears.

"My compliments to Olivia," I said. I rubbed the top of her head before walking into the kitchen where the rest of my family was mid-breakfast.

"Pancakes, Eden?" Aunt Thora asked.

"There's only one answer to that question," I said, and settled next to my brother at the table.

"Aunt Eden, I had whipped cream on my pancakes," Olivia said proudly.

"That sounds like a genius idea," I said. "I think I'd like some on mine."

"Coming right up," Aunt Thora said.

"I'm glad you're feeling better," I told my niece.

"We all are," my mother said. "You've finally made yourself useful around here."

Anton's phone buzzed and he glanced at the screen. "Oh, wow. Good news. The renovations on our house are about finished."

"Thank Nyx," my mother said, but quickly recovered. "Oh, I mean what a shame. We've so enjoyed having you here."

"We'll be sorry to go," Verity said. "It's been cozy all under one roof."

"Yes, cozy," my mother repeated, and I could tell by her expression that wasn't the adjective she'd choose.

"Mom-mom," Olivia said, "you'll still see us all the time when we move out, right?"

My mother leaned over and stroked her hair. "Of course, darling. We're family. We don't leave." She paused. "Well, unless your name is Eden and you have an ego the size of Texas."

"What's an ego?" Olivia asked.

My mother gave her cheek an affectionate pinch. "Don't

you worry about that right now. You focus on your id."

Olivia frowned. "What's an id?"

My mother straightened and looked at Verity. "What are they teaching these children in school anymore?"

"The alphabet," Verity said.

My mother patted Olivia's head. "Don't you worry, sweetheart. Your father was in the slow class, too, and he turned out okay."

Verity bristled, while Anton merely seemed amused. He tended to take our mother's jabs in stride.

"If they're moving out, does that mean I can move out of the attic until the barn is ready?" I asked.

"No," my mother and Grandma said in unison.

"Why not?" I asked. "There'll be plenty of room."

"We need to keep the rooms available for their overnight visits," my mother said.

"They live locally," I argued. "They don't need overnight visits."

"The children will," Grandma said.

"And Ryan will still nap here during the daytime when his mother is too busy being a feminist to look after him," my mother said.

Verity cleared her throat and gave my mother a murderous look.

"What?" my mother asked, blinking innocently.

"We won't leave you completely empty handed," Verity said. "We'll let Charlemagne stay here. The handbook says it's vital not to disrupt a python's schedule too much."

Ooh, Verity for the win.

Olivia's lip began to quiver. "Charlemagne won't come to live with us?"

Verity squeezed her daughter close. "Now, honey. It'll be fine. Charlemagne loves living here with Princess Buttercup." I noticed she didn't mention Candy. Nobody loved living with Grandma's familiar, not even the snake.

"Olivia, you'll be here all the time," Verity said. "You won't even notice that the snake's not living with us."

Olivia sniffed. "It's not fair."

"We have to do what's best for Charlemagne," Verity said, "no matter how much it hurts us."

Princess Buttercup barked and ran for the front door.

"Bit early for company," my mother said.

"I bet it's that Michael Bannon coming to apologize," Grandma said.

"I bet it's Mrs. Paulson with more muffins," Aunt Thora said.

I pushed back my chair. "Why don't I just answer the door and we can stop speculating?"

On my way there, Alice stuck her head out of one of the walls. "It's the chief."

My stomach tightened. Was I in trouble for yesterday's chaos? It wasn't as though I could explain the situation.

I gave my shoulders a quick shake to loosen the muscles and opened the door. He stood on the front porch, wearing tight jeans and a cotton shirt that showed off his toned physique. Kill me now.

"No uniform?" I asked.

He glanced down at his casual attire. "I'm not on duty."

Well, that was a relief. He wouldn't come here to give me a hard time about the festival if he wasn't in chief mode.

A small bark beside him drew my attention downward. "Achilles," I said, delighted. Princess Buttercup pushed past my legs to greet the pug with a gentle sniff.

Please don't drip acid on the adorable pug, I thought.

"That's quite a look you've got there, Princess Buttercup," he said.

I snatched off the butterfly clip and the silk scarf. "Olivia's been playing dress-up with the pets lately. Her new obsession."

"At least she's moved on from you."

"Seems to be the general trend," I said, and immediately cringed.

An awkward pause followed.

"I assumed you were here to give me a hard time about the festival," I finally said.

"By all accounts, it was an unfortunate accident," he replied. "I think I know you well enough now to realize you're not running around destroying coveted displays for the thrill of it."

"You're more understanding than some people," I said.

He chuckled. "Like Mrs. Hughes? That's the mother of your ex-boyfriend, right?"

"Tanner," I said.

"Right. She tried to file a complaint, but it's nothing you need to worry about."

I inclined my head. "What do you mean that she tried? What stopped her?"

"Nothing stopped her," he said. "I let her complete the paperwork, and when she left, it might have fallen straight into the wastebasket. Another unfortunate accident."

"So if you're not here to scold me," I said, "then what brings you here?"

"Achilles has learned a few tricks," Chief Fox said. "I thought you might like to see them."

My spirits lifted at the thought of Chief Fox spending quality time with his new companion. "That's great," I said. "I'd love to."

He paused. "I could show you a few tricks of my own, as well, if you're interested."

A whirlwind began to pick up speed in my stomach. "Chief…"

He held up a hand. "Relax, I'm kidding. You've made it clear you're not interested."

"It's not that simple," I started to say, but it really was. It had to be.

"I get it, Agent Fury," he said. "We're both dedicated to our jobs and we don't want to do anything that would interfere with our respective duties."

"We're rule followers by nature," I said. "It's why we chose the paths we did."

"True, but there's no reason we can't be friends, right?" he asked. "Nothing in the rules about that."

"No, of course not," I said.

"Then how about we head to the park and Achilles will show us what he's learned?" He scratched Princess Buttercup behind the ear. "Her Majesty, too."

The hellhound barked in response. I knew what her answer was.

"I guess that wouldn't be breaking any rules," I said.

"Oh, and I invited Corinne LeRoux," he added. "I hope you don't mind. She said she'll meet us over there. She doesn't have a dog, but she seems fond of them."

It took me a second to organize the rush of thoughts and emotions that invaded my body. "That sounds…" Awful. Terrible. Heartbreaking. "Great."

The chief grinned. "I was hoping you'd say that. Come on, Fury. Let's see if you toss a Frisbee as well as you toss the world's largest wheel of cheese."

I cast a quick glance over my shoulder to see Alice's ghostly form watching from the window. Her expression seemed to mirror my own.

I forced a smile and followed the chief to his car with Princess Buttercup trotting beside me. If this was the only way forward, then I'd stay between the lines that had been drawn for me. My name might be Fury, but I wasn't like the others. I followed the rules. I was good. *That* was my true nature and I was determined to keep it that way. I'd been a part of my family long enough to learn that deviation was a slippery slope and the cost was far more than I was willing to pay.

"Keep up, Fury," he teased. "You've got to prove yourself."

I slipped into the passenger seat beside him. "I'm trying," I said.

I really, really was.

* * *

Look out for **Bedtime Fury**, Book 5 in the Federal Bureau of Magic Cozy Mystery series!

ALSO BY ANNABEL CHASE

Thank you for reading **Grace Under Fury**! Sign up for my newsletter and receive a FREE Starry Hollow Witches short story— http://eepurl.com/ctYNzf. You can also like me on Facebook so you can find out about the next book before it's even available.

Other books by Annabel Chase include:

Starry Hollow Witches

Magic & Murder, Book 1

Magic & Mystery, Book 2

Magic & Mischief, Book 3

Magic & Mayhem, Book 4

Magic & Mercy, Book 5

Magic & Madness, Book 6

Magic & Malice, Book 7

Magic & Mythos, Book 8

Magic & Mishaps, Book 9

Spellbound Paranormal Cozy Mysteries

Curse the Day, Book 1

Doom and Broom, Book 2

Spell's Bells, Book 3

Lucky Charm, Book 4

Better Than Hex, Book 5

Cast Away, Book 6

A Touch of Magic, Book 7

A Drop in the Potion, Book 8

Hemlocked and Loaded, Book 9

All Spell Breaks Loose, Book 10

Spellbound Ever After

Crazy For Brew, Book 1

Lost That Coven Feeling, Book 2

Wands Upon A Time, Book 3

Charmed Offensive, Book 4

Printed in Great Britain
by Amazon